mc

"How can I be a mother to this little girl," Barbara asked softly in the darkness, "when every time I look at her I see...?" Her voice trailed off, the name too hurtful to speak aloud.

She was silent for a long moment, recalling the face of another child—her smiles, her laughter and tears, the bedtime ritual, the prayers, the good-night kisses. "It hurts, Doug," she whispered. "All I can see is…Caitlin, but Caitlin isn't here."

There was no reply.

This man she had loved for over ten years was closer to her than any other human being had ever been. They were one in every way that counted. Over the years, they had shared their most private thoughts and their most intimate moments.

And yet, in the silence of this moment, in the pressing darkness of their bedroom, Barbara had never felt more alone, or more in need of comfort.

Books by Carole Gift Page

Love Inspired

In Search of Her Own #4
Decidedly Married #22
Rachel's Hope #40
A Family To Cherish #88

CAROLE GIFT PAGE

writes from the heart about issues facing today's adults. Considered one of America's best-loved Christian fiction writers, Carole has completed her fortieth book, publishing both fiction and nonfiction with a dozen major Christian publishers, including Thomas Nelson, Moody, Crossway, Bethany, Tyndale and Harvest House. An award-winning novelist, Carole is the recipient of two Pacesetter awards and the C.S. Lewis Honor Book Award. Several of her novels have been nominees for the Campus Life Book of the Year Award and the prestigious Gold Medallion Book Award. Over 800 of her stories, articles and poems have been published in more than 100 Christian periodicals.

A frequent speaker at churches, conferences, conventions, schools and women's ministries around the country, Carole finds fulfillment in being able to share her testimony about the faithfulness of God in her life and the abundance He offers to those who come to Him.

Born and raised in Jackson, Michigan, Carole taught creative writing at Biola University in La Mirada, California, for several years and currently serves on the advisory board of the American Christian Writers. She and her husband, Bill, live in Moreno Valley, California. They have three children (plus one in heaven) and three grandchildren.

A Family To Cherish

Carole Gift Page

STEEPLE HILL BOOKS

ISBN 0-373-87094-9

A FAMILY TO CHERISH

This edition published by arrangement with Steeple Hill Books.

Visit us at www.steeplehill.com

Printed in U.S.A.

For thus says the Lord: "Behold, I will extend peace to her like a river…like a flowing stream. Then you shall feed; on her sides shall you be carried, and be dandled on her knees. As one whom his mother comforts, so I will comfort you...."

—*Isaiah* 66:12, 13

In memory of our own Misty Lynne Page,
who slipped so swiftly and silently
from our arms into Jesus' loving arms.

Chapter One

Barbara Logan was standing at the bedroom mirror in her silk dressing gown when her husband glanced over at her and that old familiar look passed between them. The look that said, *I love you...I need you...I want you...now.* Barbara felt the impact of that look and caught her breath. It was like the sudden dip in the road that tickles one's tummy. For an instant she averted her gaze, partly out of embarrassment, partly out of habit. Then she looked back at Doug to be sure she hadn't imagined that beguiling glance in his smoky blue eyes. But already it was gone, replaced by his usual take-charge, matter-of-fact expression.

"Did you pick up my shirts at the cleaners, Barb?"

"They're right there on the bureau," she replied, masking her disappointment. In the old days when they were dressing for a dinner party, he would have swept her into his arms and teasingly insisted they make mad passionate love before the company arrived. But these days they hardly managed to carry on an ordinary conversation without a sense of awkwardness and remoteness creeping between them. Over time the aloofness had become a wall too high to scale and too thick to penetrate. For Barbara, it was easier talking with a stranger than with the man she had been married to for nearly ten years.

Of course, Barbara blamed herself for their alienation. Too many times over these past four years she had rebuffed Doug's overtures of affection. She hadn't wanted to. She hadn't even intended to. But she couldn't help herself. Loving him brought back too much pain. Didn't he feel it, too? How could he think they could simply resume their lives after they had lost so much? But he refused to talk about it, so she didn't talk about it, either. It was as if they had silently agreed they would never discuss that one shattering, profoundly significant event in their lives.

"The Van Peebles should be here any time," said Doug, buttoning his starched white shirt. A tall, solid man with curly black hair and a swarthy complexion, Doug had an athletic build and strong, muscular arms from years of weight lifting in college. Yet he had the supple grace of a ballroom dancer.

No wonder Barbara had fallen in love with him almost at first sight that day she spotted him playing volleyball on the beach. And when he had smiled with those riveting blue eyes and invited her to join the game, she had known there was no turning back. This was the man for her.

"I told them seven o'clock," Doug was saying, "and Clive is a great one for punctuality. As he always says, 'Time is money and money, time.'"

Barbara eased herself gingerly into her black satin evening dress with its V-neckline and scoop back. "I guess all that Van Peebles punctuality comes from him being a bank president, do you think?"

"And from being one of the richest men in town," noted Doug. "Fortunately for the hospital, he's also one of the most generous."

"Thanks to you," said Barbara. "You saved his life five years ago with that quadruple bypass. He still claims you're the best surgeon on the West Coast."

"*Was,*" Doug corrected, tight-lipped.

Barbara stole another glance at him, but didn't reply. She had never understood how her husband could give up an illustrious surgical career for a dreary administrative position in the same hospital. Yet Doug seemed to have a genuine knack for fund-raising. Mercy Hospital had already added a cancer wing and begun work on a new children's wing with the money Doug had brought in.

Barbara watched as her husband put on his gold cuff links, the diamond-studded ones she had given him on their fifth anniversary, when they still believed love could conquer every obstacle. "I hope you remembered to put Tabby outside, Barb. Remember Mrs. Van Peebles's allergies."

"Are you kidding? I scrubbed the entire house with disinfectant. I never saw anyone who hated cats like she does."

"I suppose if the furry critters gave us sneezing fits like they give her, we'd banish Tabby to Outer Mongolia, too."

Barbara turned her back to Doug so he could zip up her dress, which he did automatically, his fingers lingering for a moment on her bare shoulder. "You look beautiful, Barbie," he said softly.

She turned to face him. "You, too, Doug. Handsome, I mean."

"Thanks." He nudged her chin, a fleeting glimpse of the old Doug shining through. "I guess we're ready. With time to spare. Five minutes at least."

"Not me. I have to toss the salad and check on the roast."

"You know, honey, if the roast is large enough, you can serve it to Nancy and Paul tomorrow."

Barbara fluffed her silky blond hair so that it framed her face just so, the loose curls accenting her high cheekbones. "Doug, you know I wouldn't give your sister and brother-in-law leftovers."

"Why not? They'd probably just as soon have a picnic in the park or chili dogs at some refreshment stand. Unless Nancy's into sushi bars now. You know how bohemian they are."

Barbara smiled. "A couple of hippies left over from the sixties. It still amazes me that you and your sisters were raised in the same family."

Doug nodded. "I was the bookish one, Pam the socialite, and Nancy the flower child," he said, a chuckle in his voice.

"I remember the last time Nancy and Paul came down from San Francisco. What was it...four years ago?"

"You know when it was, Barbie. Right after—"

Barbara cut him off before he said the words. "Of course I know. In my mind I can still see that sister of yours. Wearing her baby like a papoose wherever she went. Always had that baby strapped to her, front or back. Like a permanent appendage. She never thought to get a stroller like other mothers."

"Nancy just has her own way of doing things," said Doug. "Nothing wrong with that."

"I didn't say there was," said Barbara, checking her makeup in the mirror one last time and blotting her vermilion-red lips with a tissue. "It's just that she and Paul are such free spirits, you never know what to expect of them."

"Good thing they're coming tomorrow and not tonight," said Doug. "I'm afraid they wouldn't mix well with the Van Peebles."

"Oh, Doug, I don't even want to imagine such a thing," Barbara replied as she headed out the bedroom door. She crossed the hallway to the spiral staircase, her three-inch heels sinking deep into the plush turquoise carpet. Halfway down the stairs, she heard the doorbell ring.

"Right on time," said Doug, passing her on the stairs. "You go toss the salad, Barb. I'll greet them."

Barbara followed her husband across the marble entry to the carved oak doors. "I'm here now. I'll say hello."

With an expansive gesture, Doug swung open the double doors and said, "Welcome! Come right in—" But the words died in his throat as he and Barbara gaped at the trio in the doorway.

Nancy and Paul Myers, beaming smiles typical of a toothpaste commercial, stood arm in arm with their daughter, now a rosy-cheeked, curly-mopped five-year-old. "Hi, guys!" said Paul, looking like a cow-puncher in plaid shirt, leather vest, faded jeans and cowboy boots. "Surprise! Hope you don't mind us showing up a day early."

Nancy, in a floral peasant dress, her straight blond hair flowing down her back like a sun-washed waterfall, went immediately into Doug's arms. He gave her a bear hug, lifting her off her feet. "Sis, I—I never expected you tonight," he stammered.

Nancy went from Doug to Barbara for a hug, laughing as if they were all sharing an enormous joke. "You know me, big brother. Always doing the unexpected."

"Keeps life interesting," said Paul, raking back a wave of sandy brown hair. As his gaze swept over Barbara's evening dress, his brow furrowed. "Hey, it looks like you folks are ready to go out on the town."

"Oh, my, yes," said Nancy with a little gasp. "Look at you two. Dressed to kill."

"We're not going out," said Barbara. "We're dining in with one of Doug's clients."

"Not client, exactly," Doug corrected. "One of the hospital's rather generous benefactors."

"Oh, then we won't intrude," said Nancy, backing toward the door. "We'll go to a hotel tonight."

"Nonsense," said Doug. "You're here now. Come on in."

The two hesitated only a moment, then in chorus replied, "All right. If you insist."

Nancy turned to Barbara. "You won't recognize Janee. She's not a baby anymore." She turned to where the child had stood, but there was no sign of the girl. "Paul, where did Janee go?"

He looked around. "She was here just a minute ago."

Alarm rang in Nancy's voice. "Well, she's not here now!"

Both Paul and Nancy darted into the yard in different directions and began calling Janee's name. Within moments Paul was steering the reluctant youngster up the sidewalk and onto the porch. Janee, a dimpled cherub with impish, sea-green eyes and a profusion of honey-brown curls, was clutching Barbara's fat, furry Persian cat tightly in her arms.

"Oh, look," said Nancy. "Janee found your cat. Tabby must have gotten out without you knowing."

Barbara was about to explain that they had put the cat outside on purpose, but before she could get the words out, Janee set the cat down, and a terrified Tabby sprinted away into the house, taking all nine of her lives with her.

"Stop her!" cried Doug, lunging after the cat and catching nothing more than thin air.

It was too late. Tabby was gone, no doubt cowering under some sofa or table lest the little Shirley Temple look-alike in a sailor dress track her down and subject her to another breath-crushing hug.

A distraught Janee burst into tears. "I want the kitty!"

Barbara saw that the situation was deteriorating fast. "Come on in," she prompted, ushering everyone inside. "Make them comfortable in the living room," she told Doug. Before shutting the door, she took a quick glance outside to be sure the Van Peebles weren't coming up the walk.

To her horror, there they were in the winding driveway, emerging from their sleek luxury automobile—the buxom Harriet Van Peebles in a full-length mink coat and the silver-haired Clive Van Peebles in a shiny black tuxedo.

Barbara stepped onto the porch and greeted them, her smile so brittle she feared her face would crack.

"Mr. and Mrs. Van Peebles, welcome! So glad you could come."

The women exchanged polite hugs, each mouthing a kiss near the other's ear. "Are we late, dear?" enquired Harriet. "Is that why you're waiting for us on the porch?"

"Oh, no, you're right on time," replied Barbara, flustered, warm-faced. "Please come in."

Standing like a little sentry in the foyer was Janee, arms folded, tiny chin jutting out, her eyes focused on Mrs. Van Peebles's coat.

Harriet bent down and smiled. "Whose little girl are you?"

"My mommy's."

"Doug's sister's child," said Barbara. "They dropped in unexpectedly."

"I see you looking at my coat, dear. Would you like to touch it?"

Janee ran her hand over the soft fur, then looked up wide-eyed and asked, "Did you kill a little animal?"

Mrs. Van Peebles drew back in repulsion. "Kill an animal? Good heavens, child, what are you saying?"

"Mommy says bad people kill little animals to make coats."

Mrs. Van Peebles fanned herself with her hanky, her face draining of color except for the rouge on her cheeks. Barbara quickly helped her off with her fur. "I'll hang this up for you, Mrs. Van Peebles. It's an exquisite coat. Just lovely!"

Doug came striding into the foyer and greeted their guests, while Barbara hung up the coat and then steered Janee back into the living room. Doug followed with the Van Peebles and made introductions all around.

"I'll go put on extra plates," said Barbara, fighting a sinking sensation in the pit of her stomach. The night was already a disaster, and several awkward, tension-filled hours still lay ahead. "Doug, would you pour the sparkling cider?"

"Can I help, Barb?" asked Nancy. "I make a great soy-based salad dressing. Or if there's anything else I can do..."

"No, thanks, Nan. Everything's ready. Everyone, please come to the dining room. We'll be eating in a jiffy," Barbara replied politely.

Barbara invited the Van Peebles to sit on one side of the linen-draped table, and Nancy, Paul, and Janee to sit on the other side. She and Doug sat at opposite ends.

"Wow, you really went all out," Nancy marveled, gazing around. "Your best silver, china and crystal. The table looks gorgeous."

"It certainly does," Mrs. Van Peebles told Barbara. "You have a real knack for entertaining, dear."

"Thank you, Harriet." Barbara looked at Doug.

"Would you light the candelabra, darling, and ask the blessing on the food?"

Doug's prayer was short and perfunctory, not like the heartfelt prayers he used to offer when his faith and Barbara's was still alive and meaningful. He was going through the motions just as she was; it was the pattern of their lives these days.

"I'll get the salad while you eat your shrimp cocktails," Barbara said, scooting back her chair.

"I don't like 'schimps,'" said Janee, wrinkling her nose. Gingerly she held up a plump, pink shrimp between two fingers, as if it might bite. "They look ugly. Like big, fat worms."

"I'll bring you some fruit jelly," said Barbara, whisking Janee's shrimp cocktail away. She returned moments later with the jelly, a tossed salad and a basket of hot rolls.

Just as Mrs. Van Peebles placed a forkful of lettuce between her lips, she sneezed. "Excuse me," she said, then promptly sneezed again. Her husband handed her his handkerchief. "Thank you, dear," she murmured. "Goodness, it must be my allergies acting up."

Barbara glanced around surreptitiously. Where was Tabby? Surely not close enough to make Mrs. Van Peebles sneeze! But just then, Barbara felt the cat's smooth fur rub against her leg and heard the familiar purr. Pretending to reach for her fallen napkin, Barbara nudged the cat away, then stood up abruptly and said, "I'll get the roast."

She hoped Tabby would follow her into the kitchen, but the cat had already disappeared again. Barbara returned to the dining room with a steaming rib roast, browned potatoes, and a bowl of freshly shelled peas. "Eat well, everyone. There's plenty."

"This is a wonderful dinner," said Clive, helping himself to a generous portion of the roast. "Isn't it delicious, Harriet?"

She took a slice of beef and sniffed loudly. "Yes, I just wish I could taste something."

"I don't want any," said Janee, as Barbara passed the roast around the table. "Mama says we don't eat meat. She says we're veter...um, veterinarians."

"Vegetarians," corrected Nancy. "But that's okay, honey. Some folks do eat meat."

"If you don't want any roast beef, maybe you'd like some peas, Janee," said Barbara, forcing her tone to remain pleasant.

"She loves peas," said Nancy.

"Do not," said Janee.

Barbara gave the child a heaping spoonful of peas.

"Barb, are you still giving piano lessons here in your home?" asked Nancy.

"Yes, Nan. I have a dozen students."

"That's marvelous. Do they perform anywhere?"

"They give a recital at the school twice a year. It's quite an event."

"And are you still playing piano for the church?"

Barbara drew a sharp breath. "No, I gave that up quite a while ago."

There was a sudden lull in the conversation. Barbara's mouth went dry. Was everyone waiting for her to explain why she would give up playing the piano when she loved it so much?

"So, Mr. Myers, what kind of work do you do?" asked Clive, breaking the silence.

"Whatever I can get," said Paul between mouthfuls of roast beef. "I design computer software programs. Games mainly. For kids. Ever hear of Appalachian Ape Antics? Or The Elephant and the Eggplant? Or The Owl and the Octopus?"

"Can't say that I have."

"Not my best work," conceded Paul.

"Janee loves your games, Paul," said Nancy, patting his arm. "Don't you, Janee?"

Janee didn't answer. She was carefully lining her peas up in her spoon.

Doug turned to Clive. "Speaking of kids and games, I've been wanting to talk to you about the hospital's plans to complete the new children's wing."

"Oh, yes, the children's wing. How's that going?"

"Great, Clive—if we can just get the funds to finish the job."

With a triumphant little smile, Janee piled the last of her peas in her spoon. Slowly she lifted the spoon to her mouth, where it remained poised unsteadily in the air for a moment.

"Eat your peas, darling," urged Nancy.

"Don't like peas."

"Janee, your mother said to eat your peas," said Paul.

"No!" With a twist of her wrist Janee flicked the spoon away from her mouth, catapulting the peas across the table. Two landed unceremoniously in Mrs. Van Peebles's cleavage. Dead silence reigned as all eyes focused on the two small green peas nestled in the matron's ample bosom.

Harriet stared down in horror at her embarrassing dilemma. "Merciful heavens!" she murmured under her breath.

Her husband leaned over and made a gesture as if to retrieve the peas, then apparently thought better of the idea. At last Harriet carefully plucked the peas from her bodice and placed them on her plate. "I think I've had quite enough peas," she said faintly.

"I'm so sorry, Harriet," said Barbara, her face flushing.

"It was just an accident," said Nancy. "Wasn't it, Janee? You didn't mean to hit the nice lady with your peas, did you?"

Janee's lower lip trembled, but before a geyser of tears erupted, Mrs. Van Peebles again broke into a sneezing frenzy.

"Barbara, dear, are—are you sure you don't have cats?" Harriet stammered between sneezes.

"I'm afraid we do," Barbara admitted. "Tabby was outside, but somehow she got inside. I'm so sorry."

Mrs. Van Peebles looked at her husband with red, watery eyes. "Maybe we'd better go, Clive."

Doug shoved back his chair and stood up. "Please, don't go, Harriet. We'll find the cat right away and put her out."

Suddenly everyone but the Van Peebles was leaving the table and looking for the cat. Random choruses of "Here, kitty, kitty," rose from the living room and dining room, but there was no sign of the animal. Just when Barbara was ready to admit defeat, Janee came bouncing to the table with Tabby in her arms.

"I found the kitty," she trilled, all smiles.

But Tabby wasn't happy to be found. The hefty feline wriggled out of Janee's arms and sprang onto the tablecloth, knocking over a crystal goblet before jumping into the arms of a startled, swooning Harriet Van Peebles.

The evening ended shortly after that—a near calamity, but not a total disaster. At the door, as Doug helped Harriet on with her fur coat, Clive told Barbara confidentially, "Don't worry. The hospital will get the money to finish the children's wing. Harriet already made up our minds before we came. She has a warm spot for kids. And as ill-fated as this evening was, one of these days Harriet and I will have a good laugh over it. And a good laugh is worth a lot when you get to be our age."

Barbara gave Clive a quick hug. "Thank you. This means the world to Doug and me...personally."

Clive met her gaze with tender, glistening eyes. "To tell you the truth, Barbara, that's why we're doing it. And if I have anything to say about it, you know the name they'll give the new children's wing. It'll be named after your little Caitlin."

Tears blinded Barbara. The only words that would come were a whispered "Thank you."

After the Van Peebles had gone, Barbara dried her eyes, put a smile in place, and went to find Nancy who was in the kitchen rinsing the dirty dishes. "You don't have to do that, Nan," Barbara admonished. "Go to bed. You've had a long day."

"No, it's the least I can do, Barb. We never meant to spoil your party."

"It's okay. It was a bit rocky there for a while, but no serious harm done. In fact, I think the Van Peebles might actually have enjoyed themselves. At least the night was unforgettable."

"Still, I'm sorry for the way Janee behaved." Nancy looked at Barbara, her eyes shaded with contrition. "She's not a naughty child, Barb. You know that. Just curious and spunky. You must remember how impulsive and rambunctious a five-year-old can be."

The words impaled Barbara. She reeled, wounded, unsteady; she couldn't reply.

Paul entered the kitchen just then with a stack of plates. "Nan, be quiet," he scolded. "You know they don't talk about that."

Nancy covered her mouth, stricken. "Oh, I'm so sorry, Barb. Forgive me. I didn't mean anything. I just thought you'd remember how it was—you know."

Somehow Barbara found her voice. "Yes. I remember."

"Which room do you want us in, Barb?" asked Paul, setting the plates on the counter.

"The large guest room upstairs at the end of the hall. It has a bathroom connected to a small bedroom for Janee. The beds are made, and clean towels are on the racks."

Paul brushed a kiss on Barbara's forehead. "Thanks. You and Doug are the best. What time do you want us up for church?"

Barbara opened the dishwasher and began loading cups and saucers. "We haven't been going lately," she said in a small, detached voice.

"You aren't going to church?" echoed Paul in disbelief.

Barbara turned to face her brother-in-law, but couldn't quite bring herself to meet his gaze. "You know how it is, Paul. We're so busy these days. Doug and I hardly have time for each other."

"But church? You used to go every time they opened the doors. You got Nancy and me going."

"And we'll get back one of these days, too," she assured him. She turned back to her dishes, but she could still feel Paul's and Nancy's questioning eyes on her.

Barbara felt a flood of relief when Janee came bounding into the kitchen and diverted their attention. "Look, Mommy, look!" the child cried, bursting with excitement. "See the pretty bear!"

Barbara whirled around and stared at the familiar brown bear with the scarlet Victorian dress and floppy wide-brimmed hat. How had the child got hold of the irreplaceable Mrs. Miniver? Barbara snatched the bear from Janee's arms. "Give me that!"

Startled, Janee grabbed for the bear, but Barbara clutched the stuffed animal possessively to her breast. Janee stared up at Barbara, her large green eyes defiant. "I want it," she said, jutting out her lower lip.

Barbara stooped down and looked Janee directly in the eye, her temper rising. She tried to keep the anger out of her voice as she demanded, "Tell me, Janee. How did you get this bear?"

Janee's tiny chin puckered. "I got it in the pretty room with dolls and teddy bears." She turned to her mother and pleaded, "Can I sleep in the pretty room, Mommy? Can I please? Please?"

"No!" Barbara replied more shrilly than she had

intended. She was trembling, her hands cold as death. "You can't sleep in that room, Janee. It's not your room. Don't you ever go in there again!"

Janee stood her ground, a feisty little moppet, precocious, imperturbable. "Why can't I? Does another little girl sleep in the pretty room?"

Barbara didn't answer.

All she could think of was Caitlin.

Chapter Two

Caitlin's room.

At midnight, as if drawn by a force beyond herself, Barbara opened the door, flicked the light switch and stepped inside, cradling the Victorian teddy bear in her arms. The room looked exactly as it had four years ago. Other than this stuffed bear, not one item had been moved, except during dusting and cleaning. Ruffled Priscilla curtains with tiny sweetheart roses framed the windows. The canopy bed was neatly made with its downy white comforter trimmed with eyelet. A family of teddy bears was nestled together in the royal blue Queen Anne chair by the bed, awaiting the return of Mrs. Miniver, Caitlin's favorite. Barbara replaced it now, tenderly adjusting the red taffeta skirt and floppy hat.

Barbara scanned the room again with a sense of relief. Yes, everything was back in place, the way it was meant to be. The white French provincial dressing table and bureau boasted a whimsical hodgepodge of dolls and books and games. The walls were bright with a mélange of crayon drawings, the paper yellowed now. And on the bed lay Caitlin's pink ruffled nightgown exactly as she had left it so long ago.

"Caitlin, my precious baby," Barbara said with a muffled sob. "Dear God, why do I do this to myself? Why can't I forget?" She stepped back out of the room and shut the door, her hand trembling slightly as she turned the key in the lock. At least now no one could trespass and violate her daughter's memory.

The next morning, shortly after Doug left for the hospital, Barbara reluctantly joined Nancy, Paul, and Janee for their grand tour of Southern California, starting with Universal Studios.

"It's too bad Doug couldn't join us," Nancy told Barbara as they stood in the long ticket line under a scorching August sun. Paul and Janee had moved to another line to see who got to the window first, and now Nancy seemed all too eager for chitchat. "You know, Barb, I told my brother he's become a stuffy workaholic. I said, 'Doug, life is too short to spend every waking moment in some dreary office.' And don't tell me he's not, Barb. I can read between the lines. I say to him, 'Doug, you and Barbara should be out having some fun and enjoying each other.' Tell me the truth, Barbara. He doesn't have fun anymore, does he?''

''Work is his fun these days,'' Barbara admitted. She looked away, her gaze moving absently over the restless crowds waiting at the ticket windows. She didn't want to get into this conversation with Nancy. How could she explain to Doug's sister what she couldn't articulate? What could she say? *When Caitlin was alive, we were a happy family brimming over with love and smiles and good times. Without Caitlin, our lives, our home, even our love has become an empty shell.*

As if reading her thoughts, Nancy patted Barbara's arm and said softly, ''God can give you His joy again, Barb. He never takes anything away without giving us something just as wonderful in its place.''

Barbara nodded dutifully, steeling herself. She wasn't in the mood to hear a sermon now, especially from Nancy, whose boundless fervor and exuberance for life had a way of exhausting the most intrepid of souls.

''You and Doug helped Paul and me discover that truth years ago,'' Nancy went on earnestly, brushing her flyaway honey-blond hair back from her face. ''You introduced us to Christ's love, Barb, and, thank God, our lives haven't been the same since.''

''I'm glad, Nancy. Doug and I are very happy for you...''

Nancy grinned, squinting against the sunlight. ''I

bet you and Doug don't even realize what you did for us. I just wish we could return the favor."

"Don't be silly, Nan."

"Silly? I'm serious as a judge. But any gift or gesture I can think of pales by comparison. I mean, we're talking about eternity here. They don't make thank-you cards for that, do they?" Her lips arced in a whimsical smile. "Let's see. 'Roses are red, violets are blue.... Since you showed us God's love, we're ever indebted to you.' It's not Wordsworth or even Snoopy and Charlie Brown, but you get the idea."

Barbara moved forward, following the line. "Really, Nancy, Doug and I just did for you what someone else did for us long ago. We shared our faith, that's all. And now you're fine and we're fine. Everybody's fine!"

Nancy clasped Barbara's arm again. "Come on, Barb. Paul and I can both see how the two of you are hurting. We talked about it last night, and if there's anything we can do to help, let us know. We'd love to do it."

Barbara wanted to say, *Just let us be.* Instead, she forced herself to reply sweetly, "Thanks, Nan, you're the best. But like I said, we're okay."

And that was the stance Barbara clung to tenaciously over the next three days as she accompanied Nancy, Paul and Janee to Disneyland, Knott's Berry Farm and Laguna Beach, not to mention two pizza houses, four fast-food restaurants, and one kiddieland carnival in the local mall.

No one could say Barbara Logan wasn't a trooper. She'd show Nancy she could have fun if it killed her. And it nearly did. She had the battle scars to prove it—a broken stacked heel, a torn linen jacket, a lost contact lens, and cotton candy stuck in her freshly coiffed hair. She'd never walked so much in her life, nor endured so many screaming kids, head-spinning amusement-park rides, and ear-splitting rap tunes. She was positively nauseated from too many greasy cheeseburgers, spicy pizzas, and hot dogs on a stick. For some reason, Nancy's vegetarianism went out the window when it came to eating out at California's leading tourist attractions.

When Paul and Nancy and little Janee piled into their van on Thursday morning for their drive home to San Francisco, Barbara stood waving goodbye in the driveway, grinning from ear to ear like the original Cheshire puss. Privately she was relieved that they were going home and that her life could get back to normal. *I couldn't face another roller coaster or eat another kiddie meal or face another surging, suffocating crowd of frenzied tourists!*

That evening, Doug arrived home in time for dinner, no doubt knowing the coast was clear and the company gone. "So they got off okay?" he asked as he sat down at the table and spread his napkin over his lap.

"Yes, all three of them. Early this morning." Barbara set a casserole of chicken and noodles on the table and sat down across from Doug.

"I guess they had a good time," he mused, stirring a spoonful of sugar into his iced tea.

"The time of their lives," said Barbara through clenched teeth. She was suddenly angry, so angry it surprised her. Her hand almost trembled as she handed him the tossed salad. "No thanks to you, Doug."

He looked at her, one brow arching. "You know I had to work."

"Every day? You couldn't take one day off to be with your own sister who comes to visit just once every few years?"

"I was here in the evenings."

"When everyone was too tired to visit."

"All right, so I'm the bad guy. So what's new? What do you want me to do about it?"

"Nothing. It's too late. Forget it."

Doug let his fork clatter on his plate. "Don't play the sweet little martyr with me, Barb. You know *you* didn't want to be out there running all over town with my sister and her kid, either."

"No, but I went anyway, didn't I?"

"No one twisted your arm."

"I went because she's your sister, and someone in this family has to act like life is normal, no matter how skewed it really is."

A tendon tightened along Doug's jaw. "We play this same record over and over again, don't we,

Barb? We keep going in vicious little circles. When will it ever end?"

She speared a morsel of chicken, but had no desire to eat. Her stomach was in knots, her throat constricting. "If you think I like things this way—"

They were both silent for a long miserable moment. Finally he asked coolly, "So how did it go with Janee?"

"Janee?"

"Yeah. The kid who makes Dennis the Menace look like an angel. Did she behave herself?"

Barbara's anger smoldered. Doug had an infuriating way of changing the subject whenever they got too close to painful truths. "If you must know, Janee drove me up a wall," she replied. "She had me pulling my hair. I don't think I could have tolerated that child in this house for one more hour."

"Come on, Barb. She couldn't have been that bad."

"How would you know? You weren't here. And she was asleep by the time you got home."

"From what I saw of her, she's a spunky little tyke. Cute as a bug's ear. Okay, maybe a bit too mischievous for my tastes."

"Are you kidding? Paul and your sister never discipline that child. She's spoiled and impudent. Worst of all, they think everything she says and does is perfectly charming."

Doug's expression softened. "Weren't we that way, too, Barbie?"

"No. Never. All right, almost never."

"So what did Janee do that was so bad?"

Barbara inhaled sharply. "She spilled grape juice on our plush carpet. She trampled my flower beds picking roses for her mother. She ran up and down the stairs and slammed doors and did a Tarzan yell that rattled my eardrums and put her muddy shoes on my velvet sofa." Barbara's voice quavered with an onrush of emotion. "And she kept begging me to let her sleep in the 'pretty room,' as she called it."

"Maybe you should have let her," said Doug under his breath.

Barbara stared at him in astonishment. "You don't mean that."

"Don't I? Maybe it's time we let it go, Barb. Stop making it a monument or a memorial or a shrine, or whatever you want to call it."

Barbara pushed her chair back from the table and stood up, her ankles wobbly. "I'm not hungry, Doug. Will you put the food away? I'm going to bed."

He stared at her, his brows knitting in a frown. "What about the dishes?"

"Leave them. I'll do them in the morning."

He bent over his plate, scowling, and muttered, "A lot of good it does, me coming home for dinner. You just walk off. Next time I'll pick something up at the hospital."

"Fine. You'll probably find better company there, too."

"Now that you mention it, I probably will."

She pivoted and, without a backward glance, marched out of the room, quickly ascending the stairs to the bedroom. She undressed and slipped into her most revealing negligee, perversely hoping to tempt her husband just so she could reject his advances. She hated herself for behaving this way, hated the terrible dead-end course their marriage had taken, but she felt powerless to change anything. It was as if she and Doug were actors on a stage, spewing words they didn't mean, words forced upon them by circumstances beyond their control.

Barbara had felt powerless since the day Doug had told her there was nothing they could do to save Caitlin. It seemed the only power she or Doug had these days was to inflict hurt on each other. It was what they were best at. What irony that the wounded had become so skilled at wounding one another. What hope was there for healing?

Barbara was nearly asleep when she heard Doug come up to bed. She lay still, her back to him as he climbed in beside her and rolled onto his side, away from her. She felt the weight of his body on the mattress, heard the springs creak. She waited, her breathing slow and rhythmic, pretending to slumber. Would he touch her? What would she do if he did? Should she risk letting him know she was awake and needed his closeness?

Barbara's questions faded when she heard her husband's deep, steady breathing. She lay in the darkness, listening, waiting. Doug was so close to her that she could feel his warmth as he lay stretched out beside her under the covers. And yet he had never seemed more distant. And she had never felt more alone.

In the middle of the night the telephone rang, startling them both out of sleep. With a muffled snort, Doug sat up and grabbed the bedside phone. Barbara sat up, too, her mind still shrouded in the gauzy cobwebs of a dream. She turned on the lamp and tried to focus on what Doug was saying. By his tone she knew something was wrong. Terribly wrong.

"Yes, this is Douglas Logan," he was saying. "Nancy Myers? She's my sister. What? When? Good Lord, no! Where did it happen? Are they—? Yes, I'll be there. What hospital? All right. We'll catch the next available plane."

He hung up the phone and looked at her, his face drained of color, the lines around his eyes taut, distorted with shock and fear. She knew that look; it was coldly, frighteningly familiar; she had seen it a thousand times in her memory. That look had shattered her life, turned her world upside down. And now it was happening again. Her heart pumped with dread. "What happened?" she demanded.

His voice was tight, hushed. "That was the police. It's Nancy. Their car crashed just south of San Francisco."

Her skin prickled with an icy foreboding. "Oh, Doug, no! Are they okay?"

"They're in the hospital. In some little rural town. A suburb south of San Francisco. We've got to go."

"Of course. I'll throw a few things in a bag."

He nodded. "I'll call the airline."

It was amazing how in sync she and Doug could be when an emergency demanded it, she thought as she packed a suitcase, tossing in underwear, sleepwear, toiletries, and a couple of changes of clothes for each of them. She made sure she had their address book, checkbook and a credit card, and put out enough food and water to last Tabby for a couple of days.

"I've got us booked on a red-eye special out of Burbank at four a.m.," said Doug, as she ran a brush through her hair. "They'll have a rental car waiting for us in San Francisco."

Barbara and Doug said little to each other during the drive to the airport and the flight to San Francisco. Each was tight-lipped, their thoughts turned inward, their emotions on hold.

They arrived at San Francisco International shortly after five a.m. The airport was nearly deserted, with only a few passengers milling around or catching a catnap on some iron bench. The huge superstructure with its endless high-ceilinged corridors was so silent and everyone so hushed that Barbara had the feeling she was walking through a mausoleum. The only immediate sound she heard was the echo of her own heels on the hard tile floor as she and Doug traversed the long hall to the baggage carousel. After retrieving their suitcase and securing their rental car, Doug got directions, and they drove the twenty miles to St. Mary's Hospital north of Hillsborough. Again, mostly in silence.

It was nearly six a.m. when they entered the hospital lobby. Daylight was already filtering through the windows, giving the room a smudged, hazy cast, as if the darkness were reluctant to relinquish its hold. Doug went straight to the information desk and asked where he could find his sister. The receptionist checked her charts and directed them upstairs, to the third floor, the Intensive Care Unit. "Dr. Glazier is on call."

They took the elevator upstairs to the ICU nurses' station, and Doug asked to see his sister, his voice tight with anxiety and impatience.

"I'll page Dr. Glazier," said the nurse. "Please have a seat in the waiting room."

Doug held his ground. "I just want to know if my sister and her family are okay. Can't you tell me that much?"

"I'm sorry. You'll have to speak with the doctor."

Doug's tone hardened. "Listen, I *am* a doctor. A surgeon. And I want some answers. Now."

"Dr. Glazier is on his way, Doctor. Please have a seat."

Doug was about to protest again, but instead he

threw up his hands in a gesture of futility and muttered something under his breath. He and Barbara crossed the hall to the waiting room and sat down on a green vinyl couch beside a tall potted palm. Nearby stood a table with a carafe of coffee and foam cups. Barbara got two cups of black coffee and handed one to Doug. "Maybe this will help."

"Thanks. Some news would help even more," he snapped. "All I want is a little information about Nan, and you'd think I was after top government secrets or something."

Barbara thought of something. "What about Pam and Benny? I wonder if anyone's called them."

"Let's wait until we have some news to report."

Finally, a lanky man in a white lab coat approached; he had a narrow face, thinning hair, and a small black mustache. He held out his hand to Doug. "Mr. and Mrs. Logan? I'm Dr. Glazier."

"It's *Doctor* Logan," said Doug. "How's my sister?"

"I won't sugarcoat it, Dr. Logan. It's serious. Your sister has sustained multiple injuries, including a lacerated liver and spleen. We operated immediately, but there was too much damage. She'll need further surgery, but at the moment she's too weak. If she can gain some strength in the next day or two..."

"What about her husband, Paul?"

Dr. Glazier's brow furrowed. "I'm sorry. Your

sister's husband was killed on impact. A drunk driver crossed into their lane and hit them head-on."

"And their daughter?" asked Barbara, choking back a sob. "Did she make it?"

Dr. Glazier's voice brightened slightly. "Yes. She was asleep in the back seat. She sustained only minor injuries. She's in the pediatric wing. Barring any complications, we should be able to release her in a few days."

"When can I see my sister?" asked Doug.

"The two of you can see her now, but just for a few minutes. She's in module 2A."

Barbara and Doug instinctively clasped hands as they entered the small, unadorned room. In the large hospital bed lay a pale figure connected to a maze of blinking, whirring machines. Barbara clasped her hand over her mouth and whispered, "Oh, Doug, she looks so bad."

Doug approached the bed and put his hand on Nancy's arm. His voice rumbled with emotion. "Hey, sis, it's me, your big brother."

Nancy's eyes fluttered open, but her gaze remained unfocused. "Doug?" she murmured through pale, swollen lips.

"Yeah, it's me, baby. Barbara's here, too."

Nancy struggled to speak, her lips forming a faint smile. "Didn't think...you'd see me again...so soon...did you?"

"Can't say that I did," said Doug, his voice catching.

"You know me," whispered Nancy, closing her eyes. "Always doing...the unexpected."

Barbara slipped over to the other side of the bed and gently smoothed back Nancy's mussed hair. "Now we need you to get well, Nan. Show us how quickly you can come back to us, okay?"

Nancy moistened her dry lips and gazed up urgently at Barbara. "Janee? Is she...okay?"

Barbara nodded. "She's going to be fine, Nan. The doctor says she'll be out of the hospital in a few days, good as new."

"Thank God." Nancy lifted her hand weakly to Barbara. "If Paul and I...don't make it...take care of Janee."

"Don't be silly, Nan," said Barbara, forcing a smile. "You're going to be just fine."

"Promise me, Barb. Just in case. Take care of my little girl."

Barbara blinked away sudden tears. "Of course we will."

Nancy swallowed hard and groped for words, her voice growing faint. "Teach her about art...and music...and poetry. Take her to church. Show her God's love...like you showed us."

Barbara fished for a tissue in her purse and blew her nose. "We will, Nan. I promise."

"Give her all the love...Paul and I gave her. She needs...a lot...of love."

Doug bent over the bed and kissed his sister's pale forehead. "We'll take good care of her, Nan, until you're well again and can take care of her yourself. You just concentrate on getting better, okay?''

Nancy turned her eyes to Doug, her sallow skin taut against her high cheekbones. ''Say a prayer. Please.''

Doug hesitated for a long moment, giving Barbara a look that said, *Get me out of this.* She stared back unflinchingly and waited. Finally Doug bent over the bed, his face close to Nancy's, and whispered a simple, heartfelt petition for her healing. Halfway through he stopped and drew in a deep, shuddering breath. In the silence Barbara could hear the *whoosh* and *click* of the machines monitoring Nancy's vital signs. After a minute, Doug spoke again, his voice broken, the anguished words rising on a sob as he begged God to spare his sister's life.

It was the first prayer Barbara had heard Doug utter in over four years.

Chapter Three

"We've got to look in on Janee," Doug told Barbara as they left Nancy's room.

Barbara felt a tight, choking sensation in her chest. "I don't know if I can. Oh, Doug, it brings everything back."

"We've got to go in, Barb. We're responsible for Janee until—until Nancy's well again."

They were already walking toward the pediatric wing. Barbara took Doug's arm, fearing her legs might buckle. Quietly they entered the small room with its frilly curtains and bright animal decor. A nurse was jotting something on a chart. Barbara drew in a sharp breath and forced herself to gaze at the sleeping child. In the large bed with its raised guardrails, Janee looked small and pale and defenseless, like a broken porcelain doll, her head bandaged, bruises on her face and arms.

Like another child so long ago.

"Oh, Doug, she looks so bad," Barbara whispered, clutching her stomach. "I think I'm going to be sick."

"How is she doing?" Doug asked the nurse.

"The child's sleeping soundly. I don't expect her to wake for several hours. You may want to get some rest and come back later."

"But someone should be here if she wakes," said Barbara.

"Leave a number and I'll call you the moment she stirs."

Barbara looked at Janee, then nodded. "You're right. She's sleeping soundly. We'll come back later, but please don't hesitate to call."

As they headed back down the hall, Doug said, "I've got to phone Pam and Benny. They should be here."

"Then what?"

"I don't know." Doug ran his fingers distractedly through his thick, curly hair. "The nurse is right. We need some sleep. Paul and Nancy's apartment isn't far from here. Twenty minutes maybe."

"Then let's go. We'll need to contact people and...make arrangements."

Barbara waited on a sofa in the lobby, while Doug crossed the room to a pay phone and called his older sister Pam in Oregon. Barbara didn't want to hear him repeat the painful news, didn't want to imagine Pam and Benny's shock and grief. She just wanted to be back home again, with everything normal, the way it was yesterday. But then again, what was normal? Barbara's life hadn't been normal for years.

Nothing was normal without Caitlin.

"Barb, they're taking the next plane out of Portland."

Barbara looked up, startled that Doug had already finished his call. "How did they take the news?"

"The way you'd expect. Shock. Disbelief. Tears."

Neither Barbara nor Doug said much as they drove the twenty miles to the renovated Victorian house in south San Francisco, where Paul and Nancy had an upstairs apartment.

As Doug unlocked the door, Barbara murmured, "It feels strange coming here like this. Like we're trespassing."

"I know, Barb, but it's got to be done." Doug opened the door, and they stepped tentatively into Paul and Nancy's world—a quaint, cluttered apartment that embodied a diversity of styles, from traditional to modern to garage-sale chic. Floral wallpaper, dark mahogany woodwork and intricately carved cornices and moldings were counterbalanced by vinyl beanbag chairs, a leather recliner, a rattan sofa, pine bookcases, and a simulated black marble entertainment unit. Plants abounded—from ceiling to floor, on every table and windowsill: creeping ferns and climbing vines, small pots of violets and hanging baskets of petunias, and plant stands with large, leafy philodendron, all badly in need of watering.

"Your sister made an art of clutter," said Barbara, noting the books, magazines, canvases and sheet music strewn around the room. A guitar was propped in one corner, an easel in another. "I'd forgotten what a creative person she is."

"When I was growing up, she was always dabbling in something," said Doug wistfully, picking up an unfinished still-life. "Always writing a poem, painting a picture, picking out a tune on her guitar."

"And what were you doing?" asked Barbara softly as she examined a charcoal rendering of Janee.

Doug chuckled ruefully. "I was putting splints and bandages on my sisters' dolls. I even tried operating on Pam's favorite Raggedy Ann. Cut the thing nearly in two. Stuffing everywhere. Told her I was doing a heart transplant. She wasn't amused."

Barbara gave him a gentle smile. "Even then you were preparing to be a great surgeon."

Doug grimaced. "And where'd it get me?"

"You're still a great surgeon. You just refuse to see it."

Doug let the unfinished canvas clatter on the coffee table, and countered, "How did this get to be about me?"

Barbara looked away. She couldn't handle this rift today. Some other time. "We're both exhausted, Doug. Let's get some sleep and talk later."

"Okay by me. I'll grab a glass of water first." He headed for the kitchen, and she followed. It was a clean, compact kitchen with more plants in the garden window and lots of curios and handmade knickknacks on the counters. Janee's colorful drawings covered the refrigerator door.

"Looks like Janee has some of her mother's talent," he said with a catch in his voice. He turned on the spigot and ran the water until it was cold.

Barbara got two glasses from the cupboard and handed them to him. "Do you want me to fix us something to eat? I'm sure there's something I could whip up."

He filled her glass and gave it to her. "No, I couldn't eat. You go ahead."

"Maybe later." They went down the hall to Paul and Nancy's room and hesitated for a few minutes before lying down on the neatly made queen-size bed. "It feels strange being here like this," said Barbara, easing herself down so she wouldn't muss the chenille spread. "I'm too tense to relax. Maybe we should have stayed at the hospital."

Doug rolled onto his side and ran his hand soothingly over her arm. "Try to sleep, Barbie. We need our rest. We've got a long, hard road ahead of us, and we've got to be strong."

Stronger than we were when Caitlin died? she wondered silently. *How can we be strong now when we still haven't got past that loss?*

Barbara fell into a fitful sleep punctuated by vivid,

exhausting dreams. She and Doug were climbing a mountain, trying to reach Caitlin, who stood perched on a precipice, crying for help. No matter how high they climbed, there was always more rugged terrain waiting to be scaled. When they finally reached the spot where Caitlin had stood, she was gone, and they were alone on the mountain, just the two of them, buffeted by dark winds, with the precipice yawning like a black hole below them. "We'll fall unless we hang on to each other," she told Doug, but when they tried to embrace, the winds and the darkness drove them apart.

Barbara woke suddenly, her heart pounding, her face wet with perspiration. Doug was no longer in the bed beside her. An irrational fear seized her, coupled with the lingering memory of the black chasm. She bounded off the bed and rushed into the living room, her breathing ragged.

Doug sat on the rattan sofa, talking on his cell phone. "Thanks, Jim, I'd appreciate anything you could do." He hung up and looked at Barbara, his eyes shadowed with weariness. "I asked some of my old colleagues who are practicing in San Francisco to take a look at Nancy. See if they can help."

"Do you think they can?"

"They're going to talk with her physicians."

Barbara sat down beside her husband. "Did you get any sleep?"

"Enough. How about you?"

"I dreamed mostly. More like nightmares. I feel as if I don't want to close my eyes again."

Doug took her hand and caressed it gently. "I'm going back to the hospital, Barb. Why don't you stay here and try to rest."

"No, Doug. I want to go with you."

He squeezed her hand and smiled faintly. "Okay. Let's freshen up and head back."

They arrived back at the hospital just as the sun was lowering, a pale orange ball on a hazy, salmon-pink horizon. In the ICU waiting room they found Doug's sister Pam and her husband, Benny Cotter, talking with a physician.

"It's Dr. Glazier," said Doug. "He must have news."

With hushed, solemn words Barbara and Doug greeted Pam and Benny. Pam was an attractive, sophisticated brunette in her mid-thirties, and Benny, a balding, impeccably dressed man with a ski nose and a booming baritone voice. They owned a used car dealership outside Portland. Benny sold cars; Pam worked for an accountant and helped keep the books for Benny in her spare time. Doug always said they were an unbeatable team; they knew how to make money and how to keep it.

The two couples embraced briefly, then turned back to the doctor. "How is my sister?" asked Doug.

Dr. Glazier was stony-faced as he said, "Dr. and Mrs. Logan, I was just telling Mr. and Mrs. Cotter that your sister has slipped into a coma. I'm sorry. It doesn't look good."

They talked with the physician at length, Doug doing most of the talking, using medical terms Barbara couldn't follow. When there seemed to be nothing more to say, the two couples took turns checking on Nancy, who looked as if she were peacefully asleep. Then they visited Janee's room. She, too, was slumbering serenely and her coloring was better; the nurse assured them she would likely be awake and alert in the morning.

It was after nine when they went to the hospital cafeteria for coffee and a bite to eat. As she ate, Barbara's weariness deepened. Conversation around the table was sparse, forced, hollow. The four of them had never been close, held little in common in attitudes, beliefs or interests, and now it seemed even harder to find common ground, aside from this sudden tragedy they shared.

The truth was, Barbara had always considered Benny an insufferable boor and Pam a brittle, self-serving woman who could be catty and mean-spirited one moment and nauseatingly saccharine-sweet the next. Barbara always had the feeling she should be on guard around Pam, as if Pam were secretly comparing herself with others and looking for ways to undermine the competition. Such negative feelings made Barbara feel guilty and uneasy. Maybe she herself was the one making such comparisons and looking for ways to diminish Pam and Benny.

Maybe they had no idea how they came across to others. Maybe this whole undercurrent of dissension lay solely in Barbara's own mind.

That was what Doug said whenever Barbara had questioned Pam and Benny's actions or motives over the years. "What is there about Pam that makes you feel so inadequate, Barbie?" Doug had asked her after one of their rare visits. "Do you resent them for choosing not to have children because it would interfere with their freewheeling life-style? Do you dislike Pam because she's not the maternal, nurturing type? She's not you, Barbie. Why don't you just try to be friends with my sister instead of second-guessing her?"

Barbara had no answer. Maybe Doug was right. Maybe the problem was her own. And yet now, sitting across from Pam and Benny as the four of them commiserated, dawdling over lukewarm coffee and cold soup, Barbara knew her instincts were correct. She would never trust Pam and Benny with anything precious to her.

"I still can't believe this is happening," Pam was saying as she stirred cream into her third cup of coffee. "I'm not good with things like this. I just fall to pieces inside. I'm a bundle of nerves." She held her hand up, her red acrylic nails catching the light. "Look at me. I'm shaking."

"We're all feeling that way, Pam," said Doug, sipping his coffee.

Pam's voice grew shrill. "Nancy's not going to

make it, is she, Doug? You're a doctor. You know these things."

"I'm not giving up on her, Pam, and neither should you."

"And poor Paul," Pam went on miserably. "Now we have a funeral to plan. I can't do it. I wouldn't know the first thing. I hate funerals. I never go, do I, Benny?"

He nodded. "This lady will skip her own funeral—I'm not kidding."

"You don't have to plan the funeral, Pam," said Doug. "Just be available. Barbara and I can make the arrangements, can't we, Barb?"

Barbara stared into her coffee cup, biting her lip to keep from saying what she really felt.

"Would you, Doug? I think that would be best," said Pam. "After all, you and Barb have, uh, well, you know...had the experience already. You know what to do."

Barbara's stomach knotted and a sour taste rose in her throat. Yes, she and Doug knew all about funerals. Four years ago Pam and Benny were out of the country on vacation and missed Caitlin's funeral. They sent an enormous bouquet of pink roses, but never again mentioned Caitlin's name, never even acknowledged in their conversations that she had ever existed. For Barbara, that was the worst sort of betrayal.

But then, she and Doug never talked about Caitlin either.

"We can't stay in town more than a couple of days," said Benny. "You know how it is, Doug. When you're in business for yourself, you gotta stay at the helm or the ship sinks."

"Will you be leaving, too, Pam?" asked Barbara.

"It depends on how Nancy does. But Benny's right. When he's away from the dealership more than a day or so, everything falls apart."

Barbara dabbed at a water ring on the table. "The doctor says Janee will be released from the hospital in a few days. She'll need care until Nancy recovers."

Pam stared openmouthed at Barbara, then flashed a quizzical glance at Doug and Benny. "My goodness, I just supposed..."

"What?" challenged Barbara. "That we'd take Janee?"

"Well, yes," said Pam, her voice rising with a slight falsetto tone. "You'd know what to do. After all, you've had experience—"

"You can say it, Pam," said Barbara ruefully. "We've had experience raising a child."

"Yes, exactly. That's what I meant. And if you had to, um, keep Janee, well, you'd have a child again. You'd like that, wouldn't you?"

"Are you saying I'd have a replacement for Caitlin?" said Barbara thickly.

"Come off it, Pam. You can't replace a child," said Doug through clenched teeth.

Pam raised her chin defensively. "I know that,

Doug. That's not what I meant. It's just that you and Barbara are both so fond of children, I thought you might enjoy having a child in your home again."

Not on your life! Barbara wanted to shout, but she resisted the urge. "Are you telling us you don't want to take Janee?" she asked instead.

"You know us," said Benny. "Pam and I decided right up front, no kids, ever. With both of us working twelve-hour days, what could we give a kid?"

Love, for a start, thought Barbara. But a dark reality struck home. That was something she herself wasn't ready to give. She had loved one child once. She couldn't imagine ever loving another.

"Besides, you work at home, Barb," said Pam. "A child wouldn't upset your routine. You could still give your piano lessons."

"Listen, this is a moot issue," said Benny, raising his large, square hands like a referee. "I believe Nancy is going to get well, so taking care of the kid will be a temporary arrangement. You can handle that, right, Barbara?"

Barbara pretended not to hear the question. At the moment, with Nancy's life hanging in the balance, Barbara had all she could handle just sitting at this table carrying on a simple conversation and trying to keep her sanity.

Doug reached across the table and cupped his hand over hers. "No one's making any decisions about Janee tonight," he said firmly. "Let's all try to get a good night's sleep—and see what tomorrow brings."

Chapter Four

At dawn Barbara was awakened out of a deep, dream-filled sleep by the phone's shrill ring. She raised up groggily on one elbow, trying to comprehend where she was. This wasn't her room or her bed. Nothing was familiar. Then, as Doug grabbed the phone and sleepily barked hello, Barbara remembered with a spine-chilling shudder. Reality was worse than her troubled dreams.

She mouthed the words *Who is it?* But Doug waved her off, his expression grim. "Yes, I understand, Doctor," he said solemnly. "I know you did all you could. Thank you."

He hung up the receiver and turned to Barbara, his features stoic. But as she stared at him, his stony face crumbled and he began to weep. "She's gone, Barbie," he whispered.

She moved quickly over to his side of the bed and

enveloped him in her arms. His chest was bare and his skin cold to her touch. She wanted to say, *It'll be okay; Nancy just slipped away with the angels in her sleep. We'll see her again someday.* But she knew Doug didn't want to hear such platitudes now, any more than she had wanted to hear them when Caitlin died, even though they were true. She and Doug clung to each other, rocking together with a slow, agonized rhythm. The sobs rose in his chest, and she could feel them in her own breast.

They had wept like this four years ago, but then somehow they had broken apart and gone their separate ways, burying their grief where the other couldn't find it. Why had it happened that way? Why had they bottled up their tears and retreated behind separate barricades as if they considered one another, rather than death, the enemy.

"At least she went peacefully in her sleep," said Doug in little more than a whisper. "There was no one like her, Barb. She was so full of life."

"And she never wasted a moment of it, darling."

Doug nodded. "If only we could all be like her."

"Maybe that's her legacy. We can try to be."

Doug released Barbara, got up and put on a shirt, his fingers working the buttons as he said, "I'd better start making some phone calls. We've got a lot of arrangements to make."

"First you'd better call Pam and Benny at the hotel."

"I will. Put on the coffee, okay, Barb?"

"You need more than coffee, Doug. I'll fix something. Eggs. Cereal."

"Anything. I'm not hungry."

She drifted through the living room to the kitchen, her eyes moving over Nancy's things—her paintings, her belongings, all the ordinary odds and ends that defined her life. *I don't belong here,* Barbara thought. *I shouldn't be intruding. Surely Nancy will walk in at any moment and say, "Don't disturb my things. Don't dismantle my life. I'm not really gone."*

A ridiculous notion, Barbara realized as she put on the coffeepot and browsed through the refrigerator. But then, wasn't that exactly the attitude Barbara had maintained for four years—never allowing anything or anyone to disturb Caitlin's room, as if she might come back at any moment and reclaim her things?

A wave of emotion rocked through Barbara like a tidal wave. She stumbled over to the small oak table and sat down, putting her head in her hands, allowing the sobs to wash over her. It struck her that she wasn't just weeping for Nancy and Paul; she was crying again for her own daughter. Why was it that every heartache and grief always brought her back to this one, leaving her mourning again for Caitlin as if it were the very first time?

The next three days were among the busiest, the most hectic and exhausting Barbara had ever experienced. Together with Pam and Benny, she and Doug packed up Paul and Nancy's belongings, carted crates to Goodwill and put the furniture in storage. Doug and Benny notified people, handled the business matters, and made funeral arrangements, while Barbara and Pam spent time at the hospital with Janee, assuring her she would be fine and they would take good care of her.

On the third day they attended the double funeral in the morning, followed by a brief grave-side service at the nearby cemetery. They received condolences from Paul's and Nancy's many friends at a luncheon reception put on by their church; then they met with the probate attorney late that afternoon.

Jonathan Wallace, a distinguished, gray-haired gentleman with a small goatee, had been Paul and Nancy's attorney since their first year of marriage. After offering his sympathies and inviting the two couples to sit down across from his huge mahogany desk, he got right down to business. "Your sister and her husband had a living trust," he said, opening a maroon portfolio and extracting several official-looking documents. "I won't bore you with reams of details. You can read the papers at your convenience. Essentially, Paul and Nancy left a modest estate. However, they had a sizable life insurance policy which will provide a generous trust fund for their daughter, Janee. They specified that in the event of their death, Janee be placed with you, Dr. and Mrs. Logan. If for some reason you are not able to become Janee's legal guardians, they wish her to be placed with the two of you, Mr. and Mrs. Cotter."

Pam spoke up. "Mr. Wallace, we've already talked about it and agreed that Barbara and Doug should take the child. I work full-time for an accounting firm and part-time for my husband, so I'm hardly ever home. But fortunately Barbara works at home giving piano lessons, so she'll be available to care for Janee."

A tremor of alarm spiraled through Barbara's stomach. "Wait a minute. We may have talked about this, but nothing was decided."

Doug reached over and seized Barbara's hand. "What are you saying, Barb? You know Nancy wanted us to have Janee. We gave her our promise."

Barbara's alarm turned to frantic butterflies, their fluttering wings doing a number on her digestive system. If they didn't let up, she was going to be ill. "I can't," she said shakily. "I just can't do it."

"Barbara, are you saying you won't take Janee?" challenged Pam, her voice shrill. "Are you forcing her on us? You know we never wanted kids. Not our own or anyone else's. We've made no bones about it."

"I—I'm just saying—"

"I would think you'd be glad to have another little girl in your home," said Benny in his booming baritone. "Man alive, Barbara, she's the same age your girl was. What more could you ask for? I mean, is this a coincidence or what?''

Tears stung Barbara's eyes. ''My heart aches for Janee, but it's not the same, and you know it.''

''Of course it's not the same,'' said Doug, squeezing Barbara's hand. ''But Janee's all alone now. Someone's got to take care of her. It might as well be us.''

Barbara searched his eyes. ''Do you really think we can do it?''

''I don't see where we have any other choice, Barb. We'll make it work. We promised Nancy.''

''You were a terrific mother, Barb,'' said Pam, her tone now sweet and cloying as honey. ''And you'll be a great mother again. Just give it a chance. You'll see.''

Barbara had great misgivings as she and Doug drove to the hospital the next morning to pick up Janee. *How do I do this?* she wondered as they walked down the corridor to Janee's room. *How do I play Mommy to a child too young to understand what has happened, a child who wants only her own mother and father, the two people she can never have?*

''It'll be okay,'' said Doug, slipping his arm around Barbara's waist as they walked. ''You know the old saying—All things work together for good.''

''That's not just a saying. It's from the Bible,''

she said, thinking how long it had been since they had studied the Bible together.

"I know that," said Doug. "I once knew the verse by heart."

She looked up at him. "I'm scared, Doug. What if she doesn't want to go with us? What if we're all miserable together?"

"Don't borrow trouble, Barbie. It'll work out. Remember what you used to say—trust the Lord."

"I did trust Him," she murmured, "and look where it got us."

He stopped and stared at her. "What's gotten into you, Barb? You never used to talk like this."

"You know the answer to that as well as I do."

"It's my fault," he muttered. "Isn't that what you're really saying?"

"Of course not." She turned her gaze away, not wanting him to see her pain. "It's not you, Doug. It's everything."

"It's Caitlin. Always Caitlin."

"All right, yes. You're right as always. I keep asking the same questions and there's never an answer. Why would God take away the daughter we loved and give us a child we hardly know? Is He punishing us? Laughing at us? It's such a terrible irony."

"Maybe good will come of having Janee in our home, Barb. We have to give it a chance."

"That's easy for you to say. You're gone all the time. I'll be the one at home every day with Janee."

"I'll make time for her. For you. I promise."

They had reached Janee's room now. Barbara paused in the doorway and looked up at her husband, hoping his strength would sustain her, as well. They exchanged brief smiles and went inside.

Janee was sitting up in bed, cross-legged. A young nurse with rosy cheeks and French braids was helping her dress, pulling an undershirt over her head. "There you are, sweet pea. Now we have a pretty little dress for you to wear. Isn't that the cutest thing? You're going to look so pretty when you go home."

Barbara crossed the room and stood at the foot of the bed. "Well, look at you, Janee," she said in her most animated voice. She felt as if she were performing, or worse, auditioning, with her very life at stake. "Sweetheart, you look like Cinderella going to the ball."

The child looked up guardedly, her face framed with silky flaxen curls, her large cerulean eyes filled with doubt. "I'm not Cinderella. I'm Janee. I'm going home."

"Yes, you are," Barbara said brightly. No sense in telling her whose home she would be going to. She would find out soon enough.

Doug joined Barbara at the foot of the bed and drummed his fingers on the metal rail. "You know what, Janee? You're going to fly in a big airplane. Won't that be fun?"

The nurse helped Janee into a pink taffeta dress

with ruffles and lace. "Janee has been our favorite patient, Mrs. Logan," she said as she buttoned the dress. "We're going to hate to see her go."

"We appreciate all you and the other doctors and nurses have done for her," said Doug in his efficient, professional voice.

"It was the least we could do, Dr. Logan, considering what this poor child's been through." The young woman paused, a shadow darkening her attractive features. "Does she know?"

"Not everything," said Barbara. "In time."

The nurse fluffed Janee's curls. "Well, I'm going to get a wheelchair to take Janee down to your car. Hospital policy, you know. You might look around, Mrs. Logan, and make sure you have all of Janee's things."

Barbara went to the small closet and opened it. Janee's sweater hung on a hanger, but otherwise the closet was empty.

"There's a plastic bag of her things here on the dresser," said Doug. "I'll check the drawers, too."

"Most of her things should be arriving at the house about the same time we do," said Barbara. They had given away the bicycle, and toys too large to mail. They could always buy her some new things later.

Janee grabbed up a scruffy teddy bear with button eyes, which was lying on the pillow beside her. She hugged the bear tightly against her chest. "We're going bye-bye, Zowie," she chirped.

"We sure are," said Barbara, "and won't we have fun!" Maybe this wouldn't be so difficult, after all. Janee seemed happy enough to be with them. Maybe, just maybe everything would go smoothly. But a moment later Barbara realized she had assumed too much too soon.

"Where's my mommy?" Janee asked, jutting out her lower lip.

Barbara and Doug looked at each other, and she inhaled sharply. No, this wasn't going to be easy for any of them. She put down the guardrail and sat on the hospital bed beside Janee. "Do you remember what Aunt Pam and I told you yesterday, Janee?"

Janee shook her head, her eyes lowered, her long lashes shadowing her cheeks.

Barbara ran her fingers through the child's soft, shiny curls. "We told you your mommy and daddy had to go away. Remember?"

A tear slid down Janee's round cheek. "I want my mommy."

Barbara's throat tightened. "I know you do, honey." She slipped her arm around the girl, but Janee wriggled away.

"I want my mommy!" Janee said in the shrill tone that clearly preceded a tantrum. "Where's my mommy?"

The nurse returned with the wheelchair and lifted Janee gently into it. "We're going for a ride, Janee," she said in a light, singsong voice. "We're going to travel around the world."

Barbara and Doug quickly gathered Janee's things and followed the nurse and wheelchair out the door and down the hall. Outside, the nurse wheeled Janee over to their rental car, helped her into the back seat and buckled her belt.

"Do you want me to sit back there with you, Janee?" asked Barbara.

Janee shook her head and clutched her teddy again. "No, I got Zowie. He's my friend."

Barbara nodded. "Well, if you feel lonely, honey, you give Zowie a big hug."

They drove in silence to the airport, Barbara aware of a sudden exhaustion seeping into her bones. So much had happened in such a short time, and now, even though they were returning home, nothing would ever be the same again.

Once they boarded the plane, Janee seemed to perk up a little. They gave her the window seat, and she gazed out at the planes taking off and landing. "Look! All the big airplanes in a row," she told Barbara as their airliner taxied onto the runway.

"They're lined up waiting to take off," said Barbara. "They have to wait their turn."

"We line up in Sunday school before we go out and play," said Janee. "Teacher makes us be quiet first."

"That's just how it is for the planes, Janee. They don't have to be quiet, but the pilot has to be very patient."

Barbara looked at Doug, seated beside her. "Janee mentioned Sunday school, and that reminds me. We're going to have to get back into church. We promised Nancy we'd take Janee."

Doug reached for Barbara's hand. "Of course we'll go, Barbie. It's something we should have done a long time ago."

The flight attendant, a young redhead in a blue uniform, came down the aisle offering pillows and magazines. She stopped and smiled at Janee. "Would you like some silver wings to put on your pretty dress, sweetheart?"

Janee nodded.

She handed Barbara the pin. "Ma'am, maybe you'd like to fasten the wings on your daughter's dress."

"Oh, she's not my—" Barbara began, then let the words die on her lips. What good would it do to explain? What difference did it make to a stranger that Barbara must play mother to a child she hardly knew? Barbara smiled faintly, took the pin, and said simply, "Thank you."

She fastened the pin on Janee's dress, and the child gazed at it for several moments, running her fingertips along the edge of the long graceful wings. "Are these angel wings?" she asked softly.

Barbara looked at Janee and for a moment no words came. Finally she managed to say, "I don't know, honey. But I'm sure angels have very beautiful wings."

Janee's face clouded and her mouth puckered. "I want to go home."

"You're going to your new home, Janee," said Barbara, forcing a note of enthusiasm.

Janee's lower lip trembled. "I want my old home."

"I'm sorry, Janee."

"I want my mommy and daddy."

"Oh, Janee, I know you do, but—"

"Mommy and Daddy are in my old house. They're waiting for me. I want to go to my old house."

"No, honey, we can't. Your parents aren't there." Barbara groped for words. "They're in heaven with Jesus, but their love will always be in your heart."

A huge tear rolled down Janee's cheek. "I want my mommy."

Barbara started to slip her arm around Janee, but the child pushed her hand away and scooted closer to the window, hugging her teddy tightly to her chest. "We go home, Zowie," she murmured. "We go home." After a while her eyes grew heavy and she drifted off to sleep.

Barbara looked at Doug and uttered a sigh of dismay. "Do we have any idea what we're getting into? Janee's never going to accept us."

"We have no choice, Barb," he whispered. "We've got to make it work."

She laid her head wearily on his strong shoulder. "I don't know if I can, Doug. Look at us. We're as bad off as she is. How are we going to help her heal, when after all these years we haven't been able to heal ourselves?''

She felt Doug's shoulder tense. ''What do you mean, Barb? We're doing fine,'' he said gruffly. ''Why do you have to analyze everything to death?''

''And why do you have to deny that our lives have been a mess since Caitlin died?''

''Because you're wrong, Barb. Our lives are whatever we say they are, whatever we want to believe. I can't help it if you insist on wallowing in the past.''

Her tone thick with resentment, she retorted, ''Maybe that's better than shutting down my emotions and working myself to death like you're doing.''

Doug heaved a disgruntled sigh. ''Let's not get into this here. Not now. We've got enough to deal with. Right now, let's just concentrate on the child.''

Barbara didn't reply. She put her head back against the seat and closed her eyes. It was another child, her beloved Caitlin, long gone, who haunted her waking hours as well as her sleep. How could she focus on someone else's child when memories of her own lost daughter sapped her emotions and exhausted her energies? Heaven help her, what did she have left to give this needy, wounded child who wanted no part of her?

Chapter Five

Barbara and Doug arrived home with Janee just after dark. A warm summer rain was falling, thrumming the roof with a steady *rat-a-tat* rhythm. The house was dark and silent, and smelled stuffy and closed in. While Doug parked the car in the garage, Barbara walked around the living room, switching on lamps. Janee stood in the entryway looking small and uncertain, hugging her teddy.

"Where's the kitty?" she asked at last in a soft, tenuous voice.

"Tabby's staying with a neighbor," said Barbara, trying to sound nonchalant, as if this were just an ordinary evening. When Barbara had realized she would be staying in San Francisco longer than a day or two, she had called Mrs. Paglia next door to come pick up their cat. "Would you like to go with me to get Tabby?"

Janee shook her head.

"That's okay," Barbara assured her. "We'll let Doug go get Tabby. Would you like something to eat?"

Again, a quick shake of the head.

"Surely you'd like something, Janee," Barbara pressed.

Janee stared up at her, her round eyes glazed with tears. "I want to go home."

"You are home now, Janee," said Barbara, wondering if the words sounded as foreign to the child as they did to her. Who was she convincing? Surely not Janee. Surely not herself.

Janee remained in the foyer, clutching her ragged bear in her arms. "Where's my mommy?" she whimpered.

Barbara closed her eyes and drew a haggard breath. This was going to be worse than she had feared. It was a miserable, no-win situation. She went over and took Janee by the hand, then led her to the sofa. "You sit here, honey, while I go make your bed, okay?"

Janee perked up. "In the pretty room?"

Barbara bristled. "No, sweetie. In the room you stayed in when you came to visit last week. Remember? It's a very nice room, too. You'll be very comfortable there."

Janee sat down finally and stuck out her lower lip. "I want the pretty room with the dolls and bears."

Barbara felt her patience waning. "I'm sorry, Janee. That room is taken. It... It belongs to another little girl."

Janee was wide-eyed again. "What little girl?"

Barbara scoured her mind for a reply Janee would understand, but she could think of only one thing to say. "My little girl."

Janee looked around curiously. "Where's your little girl?"

Barbara sank down on the sofa beside Janee, suddenly too exhausted even to move. "My little girl's in heaven, Janee, just like your mommy and daddy."

Janee gazed up soulfully at her. "Will my mommy and daddy take care of her?"

Barbara's heart melted. "Yes, honey, just like I'll take care of you."

For a moment the two gazed at each other with faint, lopsided smiles—a mother without her child, a child without her mother. Too quickly the smiles gave way to sad faces, and Barbara looked away, the familiar pain rising unexpectedly like a geyser. She stood up abruptly and said, "I'd better go make your bed, Janee. You look like a tired little girl."

Doug came bounding into the house then, his curly black hair studded with glistening raindrops. He was carrying their suitcases and Janee's small bag. "It's becoming a downpour out there," he said, setting down the cases and running his hand over his hair. "We're sure having a wet summer." He looked from Barbara to Janee. "So are you two getting settled? Any problems, Barb?"

"No. I'm just going upstairs to make Janee's bed." When Doug gave her a sharp questioning glance, she promptly said, "In the room she had before. The little room just off the guest room."

Doug's gaze was penetrating. "I thought maybe..."

"No, Doug," she said coolly. "Don't even suggest it."

Doug loosened his tie. His dress shirt was damp with rain and stuck to his muscled chest. "I'm going upstairs, Barbie, and get some shut-eye. I'll take the cases up. I've got to be at the hospital early tomorrow. There'll be a mountain of paperwork waiting for me."

"What about getting Tabby?"

"It's late. Leave her with Mrs. Paglia. She won't mind keeping her another night."

"Okay. I'll take Janee up to her room and get her settled. I'll be to bed shortly."

"I'll try to stay awake." Doug gave Barbara a quick kiss on the lips and headed upstairs with the luggage. Barbara took Janee's hand and crossed the room, turning off the lights as she headed for the stairs.

On the way to Janee's room, Barbara grabbed a set of twin-size sheets from the wardrobe and a set of towels from the hall closet. She led Janee by the hand into the cozy bedroom. "You sit in the little rocker with your teddy while I make your bed."

When the bed was made, she opened Janee's bag and handed her a pair of Winnie-the-Pooh pajamas. "You can go in the bathroom and get ready for bed, sweetie. I'll get you a glass of water and put on the night-light for you."

Janee padded off to the bathroom in silence, and returned minutes later, still hugging her floppy bear. Barbara pulled back the covers and said softly, "Into bed, honey."

Janee climbed into the bed and lay very still, staring up at the ceiling, solemn-faced, her droopy bear nestled on her chest. Barbara tucked the covers up around Janee's neck and debated whether to kiss her good-night. She decided against it. "Good night, honey," she whispered, and flipped the light switch.

"My prayers," said Janee. "Mommy listens to my prayers."

"Of course." Barbara sat down on the edge of the bed and waited while Janee folded her hands and closed her eyes. In a small, light voice she said, "Now I lay me down to sleep… I pray the Lord my soul to keep… If I should die before I wake, I pray the Lord my soul to take."

Barbara winced as tears gathered under her lids. Those familiar words, spoken with such trust and innocence, twisted in her heart like a dagger. *If I should die…*

But Janee hadn't finished praying. "God bless

Mommy, and God bless Daddy, and God bless Aunt Barbara and Uncle Doug, and God bless Tabby, and Zowie, and..." The prayer went on for another minute or so as Janee surely named every person she had ever met. When she finally said "Amen," Barbara joined her, echoing the sentiment. "Now it's time to go to sleep, Janee. I'll be down the hall if you need me."

"Aunt Barbara?"

"What, Janee?"

"When will my mommy and daddy come get me?"

Barbara caught her breath, suddenly weak-kneed. "They can't come, sweetie. But someday you'll go see your mommy and daddy."

"In heaven?"

"Yes, honey. In heaven."

Janee's voice wavered. "No! I want Mommy and Daddy to come here."

"Oh, honey, they would if they could. They love you very much." Impulsively Barbara knelt and brushed a kiss on the top of Janee's head. The feel of the child's soft, tousled curls against her lips pierced a hidden alcove in Barbara's heart, a secret place she hadn't let anything touch in four long years. She reeled inwardly, smitten by an inrush of pain.

As a sob rose in her throat she straightened and strode wordlessly out the door. She padded down the hall to the master suite and hurried inside, shutting the double doors behind her.

Doug sat up in bed, bare-chested, his face cast in shadows, except where a small bedside lamp etched his handsome features with a golden glow. "Are you okay, Barb?"

She sank down on her side of the king-size bed and unbuttoned her silk blouse with shaky fingers. "No, Doug. I'm frazzled."

"I know, hon. It's been a long day."

She finished undressing and slipped into a sheer nightie. "That's not the problem, Doug."

"Then what is? Janee?"

"Yes." She climbed in beside him and stretched her slender limbs between the cool, smooth sheets. What a relief to be back in her own bed.

"What about Janee?" asked Doug warily, lying back down and pulling her gently into his arms.

Barbara nestled her cheek against Doug's firm chest. "How can I be a mother to Janee when every time I look at her I see..." Her words trailed off, too hurtful to speak aloud.

"I know, Barb. It's hard for me, too. But what can we do? Let's just take it a day at a time."

Barbara was silent for a moment, recalling the face of another child—her smiles, her laughter and tears, the bedtime ritual, the prayers, the good-night kisses. "It hurts, Doug," Barbara whispered. "It's like I'm going through all the right motions...with the wrong child. All I can see is Caitlin, but Caitlin isn't there."

As Barbara waited for Doug to reply, she became aware of his deep, rhythmic breathing. Was it possible? He was already asleep! She lay quietly in his arms, her head still on his slowly rising and falling chest, and let her own breathing match his. Inhale...exhale. Slow and steady as gently lapping waves of the sea.

This man she had loved for over ten years was closer to her than any other human being had ever been; she could feel the heat from his slumbering body warming hers. They were one in every way that counted. Over the years they had shared their most private thoughts and their most intimate times together. And yet, in the silence of this moment, in the pressing darkness of their room, Barbara had never felt more alone.

Sometime in the night Barbara heard a child cry out. She sat bolt upright in bed and said breathlessly, "Caitlin? Is that you?" Sloughing off the dregs of sleep, she slipped out of bed and hurried barefoot out of her room and down the hall to Caitlin's room. Her heart hammering with rabid expectancy, she flung open the door and flicked on the light. The sudden blinding glare brought her to her senses. Of course it wasn't Caitlin she heard crying. It was the other child down the hall, the tiny youngster who haunted Barbara with her similarities to Caitlin and yet taunted her with her differences.

They weren't the same child. They never could be. This tiny stranger could never take Caitlin's place. And yet, wasn't that just what Janee was destined to do—to slowly fill the spaces in Barbara's life and in her home that had been Caitlin's? As Barbara carefully closed the door to the silent, untouched room, she whispered solemnly, "Caitlin, baby, no matter what happens, Janee will never take your place in my heart. Never!"

Chapter Six

The crying came again. Janee weeping in her sleep. Barbara went to her, her own tears balled in her chest, constricting her breathing. Janee was asleep in her trundle bed, her scruffy teddy with its button eyes and pug nose nestled against her cheek.

Barbara watched the child from the doorway, fearful of making a sound and waking her. Janee whimpered and called out "Mama," her voice muffled, indistinct; then she was silent again. Barbara didn't move. What could she do? What help could she be? How could she offer Janee comfort when she was so desperately in need of comfort herself?

Barbara returned to her room and climbed in again beside Doug, fluffing her pillow under her head, allowing her body to relax against his warm, solid torso, barely touching.

Doug stirred and asked sleepily, "What's wrong?"

"Nothing. Janee's just restless. Go back to sleep."

He was slumbering again almost as soon as she said the words. She lay on her back and stared up into the darkness as splinters of resentment imbedded themselves in her heart. She was angry at Doug, and she didn't even know why. The anger had festered in her subconscious now for years, although most of the time she wasn't even aware that it was there. But at times like this, during moments of crisis, she experienced a flaring, irrational rage that shook her to her very roots. Doug unwittingly aggravated the situation by being oblivious to the crisis, or seemingly unconcerned, or disgustingly unflappable. His answer to every problem was to work harder, work longer, work until he was numb and nothing else mattered.

Barbara had hoped there might be a faint glimmer of a silver lining in Paul's and Nancy's tragic deaths. When she and Doug had wept in each other's arms, she had seen the chink in his self-imposed armor and had prayed they might somehow break through the wall that had separated them since Caitlin's death, that they might topple the barrier that had left them both languishing in emotional isolation.

But already Doug's tears were dried and he was switching back into his detached, professional mode. The transformation was evident; he was sleeping soundly again, as if he hadn't a care in the world. Barbara's window of opportunity was gone. Again.

When Barbara woke in the morning, she rolled over and felt for Doug, but his side of the bed was empty. She sat up and looked around and realized he had already left for the hospital. That meant she was left alone for the day to deal with Janee. She searched her mind to recall what sort of routine she had followed years ago with Caitlin. Those days seemed so long ago. What were they like? What were mornings like? She had tried so hard to forget; now the memories were buried too deep to recall.

No, wait. She remembered. Caitlin had often come running into their room at the crack of dawn and jumped into bed, right in the middle between her and Doug. Caitlin would chortle as if she were playing a wonderful game. Sometimes she and Doug would have a pillow fight, while Barbara warned them to be careful not to break something, and sometimes they both turned on her and she had to duck away from the pillows. They laughed so easily in those days. Happiness was so readily taken for granted.

Not anymore. Happiness was no longer a single-hued emotion; these days it was bittersweet, mingled with pain.

Barbara showered and dressed and went downstairs to the kitchen to fix oatmeal. Oatmeal was good for a child. Or maybe Janee liked only the airy, sugary-sweet cereal that came in bright colors and the shapes of hearts and diamonds and stars. Or maybe Nancy, with her flower-child mentality, had fed Janee granola or some other health food concoction. Barbara decided she would try Janee with the oatmeal first.

She was about to go upstairs to wake the child when she heard a little voice behind her. Barbara whirled around to see Janee standing in the doorway in her pajamas, her spun-gold curls tousled, her blue-green eyes looking up expectantly. Her teddy bear hung limply from one hand. "I go home now," she said softly.

Barbara's heart lurched and tears came unbidden. Janee, with her rosy cheeks and dimples, was a precious little girl…just not the right little girl. Barbara knelt down beside her and looked into her eyes. This could have been Caitlin. Should have been Caitlin. "I'm sorry, honey. You can't go home. This is your home now."

"No!" Janee retorted. "I go home. I fly in a big airplane."

"Not today, sweetie." Barbara straightened and took Janee's hand. "I made you some oatmeal. Do you like it with brown sugar?"

"I want crunchy cereal with marshmallows."

"I'll have to take you shopping, and you can show me the things you like, okay?"

"We go shopping now?"

"No. Later. I have piano students coming soon.

Would you like to learn how to play the piano, Janee?"

The child shook her head emphatically.

"Well, maybe you'll change your mind someday. Now if you don't want oatmeal, maybe you'd like some cocoa and toast. That's what my mother used to make for me. She'd cut the toast in three long strips so they'd be easy to dunk."

Janee's interest perked. "Where's your mommy?"

Barbara hesitated. "My mother is in heaven."

"With my mommy?"

"Yes, honey. With your mommy."

"I want to go to heaven, too."

"Someday you will."

"When? Today?"

"No. It'll be a long, long time, sweetie."

"Will my mommy wait for me?"

"You bet she will. She'll be waiting with Jesus. He loves you and He loves your mommy."

Janee seemed mollified for the moment. "Where's my cocoa and toast?"

"We'll fix it right now. I'll let you help me."

Somehow Barbara got through breakfast with Janee. They sat across from each other, eating in silence, neither quite comfortable yet with the other. Afterward, Barbara helped Janee bathe and wash her hair, even though the child insisted she could do it all by herself. After the bath, Barbara unpacked Janee's suitcase and picked out a pretty pink dress for her to wear, but Janee was already pulling on a rumpled T-shirt and jeans.

Oh, well, let her wear what she pleases. Barbara's arms and legs ached from bending over the tub and washing Janee's curly locks. She had forgotten how exhausting caring for a child could be. Wearily she led Janee downstairs to the family room and turned on the television set to a puppet show. "Would you like to watch the puppets while I straighten the kitchen and get ready for my students?" she asked brightly.

Janee shook her head. "I want my favorite show, with the little doggies."

"I don't know what show that is, honey. You'll have to watch this one for now."

"I don't like this one!"

"Just watch it for a few minutes, sweetheart. Then we'll look for one you like better."

Already Barbara was feeling a stab of guilt. She had always looked with a modicum of contempt upon parents who allowed the television set to become a baby-sitter. *But after being away from home for so long, I've got a million things to do,* Barbara reasoned. She couldn't spend the entire day entertaining the child.

Roger Gibbons, her first student of the day, arrived just as Barbara was loading the dishwasher. A talented, serious-minded twelve-year-old, Roger was one of Barbara's most promising students. She left the dishes in the sink, made sure Janee was still sitting cross-legged on the floor in front of the television set, then joined Roger at the piano. She felt a bit harried and unprepared, but that was probably because she hadn't taught in over a week. She would be fine once she was into the lesson.

Barbara was in the middle of teaching Roger *arpeggios* when she felt a small hand tug on her sleeve. "I want a drink."

Barbara looked around at Janee and said, "In a minute."

"I'm thirsty," Janee persisted.

"Practice for a minute," Barbara told Roger. She went to the kitchen, ran the tap until the water was cold, and filled a small glass for Janee. "Be careful not to spill it," she cautioned. She had just returned to the piano when she heard glass shattering in the kitchen. She dashed back and found Janee standing on the wet linoleum with shards of sparkling glass at her feet.

"It fell down," she whimpered.

Stepping carefully, Barbara reached out and lifted Janee into her arms. "Thank goodness, you're wearing tennis shoes." She carried Janee back to the family room, examining her hands and arms for cuts. "Are you okay? No hurts?"

"No ow-wees," said Janee.

"Keep practicing," Barbara called to Roger as she headed back to the kitchen to clean up the mess.

If Barbara had assumed her day could only get better, she was sadly mistaken. By mid-afternoon, as she greeted her last student, a tall, gangly fourteen-year-old girl named Alice Dubuis, Barbara was ready to pull her hair out. Janee had managed to disrupt every lesson. Either she was hungry or thirsty or tired of watching television or she had a tummy ache or was too warm or too cold or wanted to know when she could go home.

Finally, while Alice practiced her scales, Barbara took Janee upstairs to her room, sat her down at the small writing desk and handed her a coloring book and crayons. "You color until I finish this lesson. Then you can help me fix dinner."

Janee looked up at her with a sullen, pouty face, her lower lip nearly dragging the floor. "I don't wanna color."

"That's too bad," said Barbara, barely suppressing her irritation. "Color anyway."

Barbara returned to the piano lesson but was too distracted to give Alice the help she needed. She ended the lesson early, promising to give the girl more time next week.

While the house was momentarily quiet, Barbara went to the kitchen, whipped up a meat loaf and put it in the oven to bake along with three large russet potatoes. Guilt nudged her as she climbed the stairs and walked quietly down the hall to Janee's room. She had promised Janee that she could help with dinner. Well, there was still a salad to toss and a loaf of sourdough bread to bake. Or maybe Janee could shell some peas. Creamed peas were a safe choice now that the buxom Mrs. Van Peebles wasn't dining with them.

Barbara opened the door to Janee's room and peeked in. "You can come downstairs with me now, Janee. I'm finished with my lessons. Would you like to help me shell some—" She broke off. "Janee?" The child was nowhere in sight.

Barbara crossed the room to the adjacent bathroom and knocked lightly. No answer. She opened the door a crack. No Janee. Maybe the child was back downstairs in the family room watching television. Barbara went downstairs and checked, but the television was off and there was no sign of Janee.

Barbara moved more quickly now, checking every room, calling Janee's name. It was ridiculous that she couldn't find one little girl in this large, silent house. Was it possible that Janee had gone outside? Barbara always kept the doors locked, but a five-year-old would know how to turn the lock. Barbara opened the double doors and stepped out on the sprawling, vine-covered porch. She looked up and down the wide boulevard, her eyes scanning the neat green lawns that flanked the sidewalk and street, intersected only by narrow, white-picket fences.

Janee was nowhere to be seen.

Barbara's pulse quickened with alarm. Janee had said over and over that she wanted to go home. Could she have gone outside and started walking down the block, determined to find her way home? Barbara shivered, her anxiety growing. Anything could happen to a small child wandering around alone. Janee knew no one. She would have no idea where she was or where to go. She would be defenseless against any stranger who happened by.

Barbara went back inside and hurried to the phone, trembling now. She would have to call Doug and tell him what happened. What on earth could she say? *I'm sorry, darling, I lost your little niece the first day she was left in my care. I just turned my back and it's like she dropped off the face of the earth.*

Barbara placed the receiver back in its cradle. No, she couldn't call Doug and worry him. He had enough grief to deal with. Perhaps the police. She could dial 9-1-1 and tell them her child was missing. Not *her* child, actually. Her dead sister-in-law's child. But already she realized how improbable the whole story sounded.

Something in her head said, *Check the house again. One more time. Maybe you overlooked some little hiding place that would attract a small child.* Breathlessly Barbara retraced her steps, searching each room downstairs, then exploring the upstairs again—Janee's room, the guest room, the bathrooms, the master suite. There was only one room she hadn't checked.

Caitlin's room.

But that was locked.

Or was it?

Barbara went to the white frame door and turned the knob, her heart rate accelerating, her mouth dry. There was an odd, stale taste at the back of her throat—the moldering taste of grief. She swung the door open and peered into the familiar room with its ruffles and lace, its dolls and bears.

Barbara's breath caught in her throat. There in the canopy bed, wearing the ruffled pink nightgown and snuggled like a kitten on the white comforter lay Janee, fast asleep. For a long moment Barbara didn't move. She couldn't be sure it wasn't Caitlin. If she moved, if she spoke, she would shatter this moment, and if it were Caitlin, she would lose her again, like a mirage, this wraithlike figure in the mists of her memory.

Please, dear God, let it be Caitlin!

As quickly as the prayer formed in Barbara's mind, she chided herself for her foolishness. Of course, it wasn't Caitlin. Caitlin was dead. This was Janee, someone else's child, a stranger in her home, who was taking over, who would slowly, inevitably erase Caitlin's memory, who had already intruded on and violated Caitlin's possessions, her very room.

"Janee! Get up! Do you hear me? This isn't your room!" Barbara cried.

The child woke and scrambled off the bed, then padded toward the door, looking dazed and confused as she rubbed one eye. Barbara caught Janee's hand, stopped her and pulled the ruffled nightgown off over her head. "Janee, you know you aren't supposed to come in this room," she scolded. "Don't you ever come in here again."

Janee's face grew pinched and she let out a wail. "I—I want my mommy," she cried.

Barbara's outrage withered into shame and regret. She picked Janee up in her arms and carried her out of the room. "I'm sorry, honey. I didn't mean to yell at you. It's okay. We're both feeling very sad."

Janee wriggled out of Barbara's arms and ran down the hall to her room, slamming the door shut. Barbara started after her, then paused and shook her head, a sense of futility spreading through her bones, leaving her exhausted. What good would it do to go after the child? What could she possibly say to make things right? What hope was there for this broken, mismatched family, anyway? Solomon said it best. *Vanity of vanities. All is vanity.*

Barbara trudged downstairs to the kitchen and checked the meat loaf. It was getting dry and the skins of the baked potatoes were growing tough. Doug should have been home a half hour ago. Why did she bother fixing dinner when she never knew when or if he'd be home to eat it?

She was grousing inwardly over her husband's tardiness when she heard the front door open and close. She quickly removed the meat loaf from the oven and set it on the counter, then forked out the potatoes, one by one. Then she fluffed her hair and caught her reflection in the microwave door. She looked a sight, but there was nothing she could do about it now. She was about to head for the foyer when Doug met her in the kitchen doorway.

"Sure smells good in here," he said with a weary smile. He brushed a kiss on her lips, then loosened his tie. The spicy scent of his aftershave lingered in the air, awakening Barbara's senses, stirring faint filigrees of memory. She wished he would take her in his arms and hold her and whisper words of comfort and make her pain go away. But she promptly dismissed the thought, for if anyone needed comfort now, it was Doug, and she was too thin emotionally to offer it.

"So how'd your day go?" he asked, shrugging out of his navy, double-breasted jacket. He hung the coat on the back of a chair and pulled off his tie.

"It was okay," she said, her tone noncommital, without enthusiasm. "How about you?"

"Hectic. A mountain of paperwork, as I expected. Everybody wanting something. Wanting it yesterday. But what can I expect? I was gone for a week. The rest of the world doesn't grind to a halt just because our lives were put on hold."

Barbara carried the meat loaf over to the table. "Maybe you can relax a little tonight." She poured two glasses of iced tea and one small plastic glass of orange juice. "One of our favorite films is on TV—that romantic picture we saw three times when we were dating. You always said I looked like the girl...."

He chuckled. "And you said I was a dead ringer for the guy. Yeah, I remember. But I can't tonight. I brought home reams of paperwork."

Barbara looked at him, exasperated. "When will it ever end, Doug? When will we ever have our lives back?"

"I don't know, Barb. I honestly don't know."

"The way things are going, everything just gets more complicated. We're on a treadmill and we'll never get off. We don't even have time to have an honest-to-goodness fight."

He managed a wry smile. "Is that what you want, Barbie? A fight? Put up your dukes. I'll take you on." He assumed a fighter's stance and did a little shadow-boxing number with his feet. "Is this what you want—a few rounds in the ring?"

Barbara laughed in spite of herself. "Oh, Doug, I wish it were that simple."

"Why can't it be, Barb? Simple, I mean. Why do we always have to overanalyze?" He reached for her, pulled her into his arms and nuzzled her hair with his chin. "The truth is, I don't know how to change things, Barb. How do we make things good between us again? I don't have the answers. And, God help me, I don't have the time or energy to find the answers. Do you?"

"I wouldn't know where to begin. Especially now, with Janee here."

Doug held her at arm's length. "What about Janee? How'd she do today?"

"It was touch and go," Barbara conceded. "I got upset with her."

"What'd she do?"

"I found her in...Caitlin's room. Sleeping in Caitlin's bed. Wearing Caitlin's nightgown."

Doug heaved a sigh. "Does it really matter, Barb? After all this time?"

Tears stung her eyes. "It matters to me. It always will. I can't help it, Doug. I can't change how I feel."

"So is it going to work out? With Janee, I mean."

Barbara blinked rapidly and looked away. "I don't know. It'll take a period of adjustment. For both of us."

"For all of us," he agreed. "But we'll manage somehow. I've got to believe that, Barb. Maybe we can do something with Janee this coming weekend. Take her to the zoo or the park or something."

"And what about church?" asked Barbara. "Are we taking her to church?"

"We promised Nancy."

"Are you up to facing Reverend Schulman? It's been nearly four years."

"Maybe he never noticed we were gone."

"Are you kidding, Doug? After all the cards and notes he sent us, and the phone calls every few months? He'll probably string a banner across the narthex and announce our return from the pulpit."

"He wouldn't."

"Wouldn't he?"

"I guess we'll find out—this Sunday."

* * *

While Reverend Schulman didn't announce their return from the pulpit, he did shake their hands heartily before the service and tell them how happy he was to have them back. He expressed his condolences over the deaths of Doug's sister and her husband, and wished Doug and Barbara great success in raising Paul and Nancy's daughter. "If any couple knows how to bestow love on a child, it's you two," he assured them. "And now God's given you another chance."

Barbara didn't agree with the reverend's sentiments, but she wasn't about to contradict him. After all, he always managed to get in the last word. And, sure enough, when he stood up to deliver the morning message, Barbara had a feeling he was speaking directly to her and Doug.

"Jesus is our great comforter," he declared in a voice that rang with passion and conviction. "He came to heal the brokenhearted, to bind our wounds, to bear our griefs and carry our sorrows. He will dry all our tears and walk with us through the darkness, if only we open our hearts and let Him in.

"Some of us have closed the doors of our hearts. We've stopped trusting Him. We have the mistaken idea that God somehow delights in inflicting pain, and we're afraid if we put ourselves in His hands, He'll take away what little we still possess.

"Beloved, nothing could be farther from the truth.

Jesus came to bring us life and to conquer death. He bore the sorrows of an entire world. He carried the burden of your sin on His back. All because He loves you with a vast and boundless love. He seeks your love in return. His arms are open wide. Let Him embrace you and heal your heartaches. Let Him whisper His comfort in the darkest night. You'll know no peace, no joy, until you give Him your heart, your life, all you hold tightly in your hand this day."

Barbara stole a glance at Doug. His expression was granitic, his eyes shadowed and unreadable. Years ago, when they sat together in church, they would hold hands like lovesick teenagers. She never tired of feeling the warm, solid grip of his hand enveloping hers.

But today he sat with his arms crossed, his shoulder hardly touching hers, as if he were warding off anyone's attempt to break through his stalwart veneer and glimpse the deep well of pain underneath. Doug was a proud, stubborn, self-reliant man. He wasn't about to open his bruised heart to Barbara, nor to Reverend Schulman, nor even to God.

The only hint of emotion her husband had shown that morning was when he dropped Janee off at her Sunday school class. The child had impulsively thrown her arms around his neck and begged him not to leave her. He had gently extricated himself from her embrace, but not before a tear slid down his cheek.

Barbara had turned away, resentful that this child her husband hardly knew prompted a show of emotion, while Doug kept four years of grief over his own daughter locked in a secret place Barbara was never allowed to see.

Caitlin's death had struck the first near-fatal blow to their marriage. Would this child strike the final one?

Chapter Seven

Janee sat looking out at the rain, her fingers pressed against the window, as if they would break through the barrier and discover another world—something magnificent, a wonderland. She stared at the rain with wide, astonished eyes, saying nothing. Just watching.

"Janee, keep your hands off the glass," Barbara prodded gently. "We don't want smudge marks, do we?"

Obediently the child removed her hands. A flicker of shame crossed her face, but her eyes remained unblinking. Janee said nothing; it was an accusing silence. To break the awkward stillness, Barbara said, "Would you like some bread and butter?"

A quick shake of the head.

"No? Well, maybe some yogurt...or cookies and milk?" Barbara let her words drift off. Janee wasn't listening. Already the child had pressed her face back to the window, to the soft pattering rain. Tabby lay stretched out beside her on the overstuffed chair, sleeping contentedly, her whiskers twitching as she dreamed.

The room was dark, moving with soft shadows. Janee sat framed by the curtains. The shallow September light that penetrated the window effused a dusky halo around Janee's wheat-colored hair.

Barbara sat across the room on the sofa, sewing a button on one of Doug's dress shirts. She felt vaguely guilty now, and yes, even a little angry. Janee's increasing lack of response perplexed her. She had been in Barbara's home for over a month now, and yet every day she seemed to grow more distant, more unresponsive, more sullen. What kind of child was she that she never said anything, never showed any feelings at all?

Barbara nodded hopefully toward the TV set. "Honey, do you want to watch television?"

Janee looked around, moving her head with a deliberate slowness; her mouth froze into a pout. "No, I don't want to watch television," she said.

Barbara tossed Doug's shirt aside on the couch and went to the kitchen to check the pot roast for supper. Lifting the lid so that quick curls of steam escaped, she noticed that her hand trembled. She let the lid fall back into place with a clatter and stared at her hands.

Janee's doing this to me, she thought dismally.

Barbara glanced at the wall calendar. In the month since they had brought Janee home, each day had seemed harder than the day before. Barbara had tried enrolling Janee in kindergarten, but Janee refused to go. Barbara had driven her to the school anyway, but Janee cried and refused to stay. Plaintively the child argued, "If I'm at school, my mommy won't know where to find me." At last the teacher suggested Barbara try enrolling her again in January after she'd had more time to accept her parents' deaths, and her new surroundings.

But Janee seemed no more content at home than she had at school. Every day she grew more silent and withdrawn. Nothing Barbara said or did seemed to help. The emotional breach between them only widened. But what did Barbara expect, trying to mother someone else's child?

It wasn't as if she hadn't tried to reach Janee, to make the child feel comfortable in her new home. But there was no way Barbara could be a mother to Janee or make up for the child's terrible loss.

And, of course, Janee didn't make things any easier. She refused every offer of affection. She no longer wanted to be tucked into bed at night, nor would she say her prayers for Barbara. She turned her face to the wall when Barbara leaned down to kiss her good-night.

Barbara returned to the living room in time to catch Janee at the front door, trying to turn the knob. "What are you doing, honey?"

"I go outside."

"No, Janee. It's raining."

Janee held her ground. "It stopped."

Barbara glanced out the window. Janee was right. The rain had stopped, and faint streamers of sunlight were rippling across the silvery sky. Maybe it would be a nice day, after all. "Okay, honey, you can go outside, but I'm coming with you. Stay in the front yard where I can watch you from the porch."

"Can I ride my tricycle?"

The trike was on the porch, shiny new and bright blue, a gift from Pam and Benny. The sight of it gave Barbara the shivers. It reminded her of Caitlin's little bicycle that had ended up as twisted wreckage under an automobile's front tire.

"Wouldn't you rather color or play with your dolly?" Barbara prompted.

Janee's lower lip jutted out. "I go ride my new tricycle."

"All right. I'll carry it down the steps for you, but be careful. Stay right on the sidewalk. I'll be right here watching."

Barbara stood watching from the porch as Janee pedaled back and forth on the wet, glistening sidewalk. *She'll be okay,* Barbara told herself. *Not every child dies playing in her own front yard.*

Barbara sat down on the porch swing and tried to relax, but even when she wasn't with Janee, the child was there in her mind, a nagging worry, a constant responsibility. Why did God expect her to take care of another child when she hadn't managed to keep her own child from harm?

Barbara was just thinking of slipping inside and checking the roast again when she heard the scream.

She sprang to her feet and bolted down the steps, visions of Caitlin's bicycle accident exploding behind her eyes.

Trembling, her ankles weak, Barbara stumbled across the soggy lawn where the tricycle was overturned and Janee lay crumpled on the rain-slick ground, sobbing, her knee badly skinned. Impulsively Barbara sank down on the wet grass and gathered Janee into her arms and held her, her own senses so stunned she couldn't be sure whether she was holding Caitlin or Janee. It felt like Caitlin, could so easily have been Caitlin. Not quite realizing what she was saying, Barbara murmured into the child's hair, "There, there, baby. It's okay, darling. Mommy's here."

The eerie magic of the moment shattered.

Fiercely Janee squirmed out of Barbara's embrace and cried, "I'm not your baby. You're not my mommy. I hate you!"

Barbara watched, stricken and numb, as the child scampered back into the house. Her own senses reeling, Barbara followed her inside in time to hear Janee's bedroom door slam shut upstairs.

Within moments Barbara realized it couldn't have been Janee's door slamming. The sound was closer. Was it possible? Caitlin's room?

A dark premonition filled Barbara's heart as she ran upstairs and strode breathlessly down the hall. As she turned the knob, she thought, *I've grown complacent, leaving Caitlin's door unlocked.* As the door swung open, her eyes settled on Janee across the room, yanking the Victorian teddy bears out of the Queen Anne chair, one by one.

"Stop it!" Barbara commanded.

With a look of defiance, Janee picked up Mrs. Miniver and held the Victorian bear over her head.

"Don't! Put it down, Janee!"

Janee stuck out her lower lip. "I don't have to."

"Yes, you do," countered Barbara hotly. "I told you to. Now do as I say, or I'll—" Her words faltered, the threat left unfinished. What could she possibly do that she hadn't already tried?

Her lower lip trembling, Janee threw the bear to the floor. Before Barbara could react, Janee ran her arm along a shelf of toys and books, sending everything cascading to the ground. "I hate this room!" she cried tearfully.

Barbara bounded across the room. She took hold of Janee's arm, her own hand trembling. "Stop it! You're being a naughty girl!"

"I hate you!" Janee cried again, wriggling free of Barbara's grip. She swung her small, chubby hand and sent another shelf of toys careening to the floor. "I hate your little girl's room! I hate her toys! I hate her!" Janee swept her arm across the desk, toppling several dolls, their lacy crinolines and scarlet taffeta skirts forming a rumpled heap beside the bed.

In one quick, impulsive sweep, Barbara caught Janee up in her arms and held her, kicking and screaming. "I want my mommy!" Janee wailed, thrashing her legs, grazing Barbara's shins. "I want my mommy!"

Barbara held Janee more tightly, determined to restrain the child, to quiet her, even though her own arms ached and her legs felt the blows of Janee's rubber sneakers. When Barbara could stand no longer, she sank down wearily on Caitlin's bed, embracing the warm, thrashing child until Janee's tantrum gave way to desolate sobs. Holding the youngster against her breast, Barbara let her own tears fall on Janee's mussed hair. They were at an impasse, she and Janee. They each desperately wanted something they could never have, and in their separate, lonely grief they were making each other miserable.

"What are we going to do?" Barbara whispered, her voice heavy with hopelessness. "What are we going to do, baby?"

Janee was whimpering softly now, almost quiet. Her clammy body grew lethargic, heavy in Barbara's arms. After several minutes Barbara heard the quiet rhythm of slumber. She stood and lifted Janee in her arms, careful not to awaken her. She carried her down the hall to her room and laid her gently in her bed.

Barbara returned to Caitlin's room and tenderly

returned each doll to its place on the desk and each stuffed animal and toy to its proper shelf. As she smoothed Mrs. Miniver's flaming red skirt, she thought, *Why am I doing this? Caitlin's not coming back. I'm as pitiful as Janee, waiting for someone who can never come home.*

Janee slept until lunchtime. Shortly after noon she trudged downstairs looking like a sad little raga-muffin. She sat at the kitchen table eating her peanut butter and jelly sandwich in stony silence. When Barbara offered her an ice cream cone, Janee looked up and nodded, her eyes tear-filled.

Barbara made a cone, handed it to her, and asked, "Do you want to go watch cartoons?" Janee nodded and scurried off to the family room. An uneasy truce settled over the household after that, but Barbara wasn't sure how much longer she could endure Ja-nee's silent, reproachful glances.

Dear God, where do we go from here? she prayed silently, adjusting the flame under the roast. *Help me, Lord. I'm at my wits' end. Janee constantly reminds me of Caitlin and what I've lost. It was bad enough before, not having my precious daughter. But now, with this child who grows to hate me more every day, it's like rubbing salt in the wound. And Janee's miserable, too. She'll never accept me as her mother. Dear God, why are You doing this to us?*

On impulse Barbara picked up the phone and di-aled Pam and Benny's number. She needed to hear a reassuring voice, even theirs. She shuddered to think that's how desperate she had become. She didn't really expect them to be home, so when Pam answered, Barbara swallowed hard and groped for words. "Pam, it's me, Barbara. I just wanted to, uh, thank you for the tricycle you sent Janee. The toy store delivered it a couple of days ago. Yes, she loves it."

They chatted a while about silly, inane things before Barbara broached the real reason for her call. "Listen, Pam, I've been thinking about something...I'd like you and Benny to consider taking Janee. Yes, I know you thought everything was settled, but, well, maybe you could just try it for a few weeks. I know you're both working, and I wouldn't even ask, but—"

Barbara's mouth went dry and her voice broke. She hated the groveling sound in her voice that Pam always inspired, but she blundered on anyway. "I'm sorry, Pam, it's just that Janee doesn't seem to be settling in the way we hoped. If anything, she's growing more distant every day. I can't help thinking maybe she'd be happier with you. Yes, I know it's a lot to ask. You don't have to give me an answer now. Just think about it, okay?"

As soon as Barbara hung up the phone, doubts and guilt came flooding in. Why had she even called Doug's sister? She knew better than to expect sympathy and understanding from Pam and Benny. And what would Doug say if he knew she had actually asked them to take Janee?

"He's got to know I can't go on this way," she said aloud, her voice sounding hollow and desperate in the silent room. "We've got to settle this once and for all."

To Barbara's relief, Doug arrived home on time for dinner that evening. No matter how painful it might be, they would have to talk. They would have to do something about Janee.

At the dinner table Barbara watched Doug, sizing up the situation, waiting for her opportunity. He was in a pleasant, mellow mood and would be in a more receptive mood still after a hot, hearty supper. With his muscular, big-boned frame, Doug was a man who relished his food, who pored over a meal, concentrating, savoring everything he ate. He was a dream to cook for, always complimenting her on her culinary skills.

But he refused to discuss anything of a serious nature at the dinner table. That was all right with Barbara. She would wait until Janee was in bed before bringing up the problems she was facing with the child.

"What about Janee?" Doug asked when she broached the subject later that evening. She had returned to her mending. He was stretched out on the couch, nearly asleep. He shook his head as if to diffuse his weariness. "What's the problem?"

"She can't stay here any longer, Doug." There!

It was out. No beating around the bush. She had said the words before she lost her nerve.

Her husband sat up startled and stared at her, his eyes narrowing. "What are you talking about? She's here. There's no question now."

Barbara moved over beside him on the couch. "Yes, there is," she insisted. "You aren't home enough to know how it's been. You don't know."

"All right. Tell me what's the matter." There was a troubled intensity in his smoky blue eyes.

Barbara twisted her wedding ring. The gold band was loose on her finger; she had lost a few pounds lately. "Things with Janee are getting worse, Doug. I've tried. Honest I have. But she has nothing to do with me. She avoids me. She's been here over a month and she's still a stranger. Worse than a stranger."

Doug shook his head ponderously. "Barbie, Barbie, you have to give her time. She just lost her parents. She's a baby. What do you want?"

Barbara leaned forward and pressed her fingertips against her temples as if she might alleviate something swelling within her skull, a pressure, a nagging irritation. "I'm being a shrew about this, I know I am," she said shakily. "I shouldn't be this way, but I can't help myself. I didn't think I'd ever feel this way."

Doug lowered his head a little, looking her full in the face, and said, "All right, tell me. Just how do you feel?"

Barbara's voice was tremulous. "I—I feel caught, trapped, a prisoner in my own house. I can't be myself. She watches me. She hates me. I feel it."

Doug scowled and slapped his knee. "That's ridiculous! She's a little girl. She doesn't hate."

"Yes, she does, Doug. She told me so herself. Today." In a halting, emotion-filled voice Barbara told him about the tricycle overturning and Janee's scream. "It brought everything back, Doug. It was horrible. I found myself reliving Caitlin's accident. I ran down the porch steps and grabbed Janee and held on to her for dear life. As if she were Caitlin. I said something about Mommy being there for her. And suddenly she stiffened and pulled away and told me she hated me. And I knew then, Doug. I knew I'd never win her over."

"You don't know that, Barb. You've got to be patient with her."

"There's more," Barbara said shakily. "After the bicycle incident, Janee threw a terrible temper tantrum. She deliberately messed up Caitlin's room. She went in and started throwing toys and dolls all over the floor and knocking things off shelves. She was like a person possessed. It was as if she hated Caitlin—a child she never even knew."

Doug shook his head, his brow furrowed. "Maybe she just wanted to play with Caitlin's toys. God knows, you've kept that room like—like a mausoleum."

Barbara bristled defensively. "I have not. I've

kept it the way Caitlin left it, as...as an honor to her memory."

Doug's voice hardened. He raked his fingers through his thick ebony hair. "Let's not get into that now, Barb. Janee was probably just angry because you wouldn't let her play with Caitlin's toys."

"It was more than that, Doug. She was willfully destructive. She didn't want to play with the toys. She wanted to destroy them. She hates everything about us and this house."

Doug reached over and smoothed Barbara's velvety blond hair. It was a tender, familiar gesture, but one he offered rarely these days. "Time, Barbie. Give her time. Time is the great healer."

Scalding tears flooded Barbara's eyes. "Time? The great healer? How can you say that, Doug?" She couldn't keep the searing words back. "It hasn't healed anything for us. We're still in the same place we were four years ago. Standing at Caitlin's grave. Waiting for something to happen, waiting for things to get better. For Caitlin to come home." The tears came with a convulsive shudder that shook her slender frame. "I can't handle another child, Doug. I just can't!"

Doug reached over, put his arm around her and pulled her against his strapping chest. His touch should have been comforting, but she sensed that he was baffled and frustrated and only trying to placate her, as he might a recalcitrant child. "I don't know what to say to you anymore, Barb. Maybe you should get something for your nerves. I could get you a prescription..."

Still playing the detached, infuriatingly rational physician, she thought dismally. Didn't Doug understand? What she needed couldn't be solved with a tranquilizer. What she needed couldn't even be put into words. She needed the tender, loving husband she once had, but he had buried himself behind the brusque, impenetrable facade of his profession. "I knew you'd think I was crazy," she sighed, slumping back in defeat. "I think it myself."

"No, honey, I don't think that. Come on. We'll figure something out."

Barbara pulled away, turning her shoulders to face her husband. She steeled herself, summoning every modicum of courage she possessed. "Doug," she began, inhaling sharply, "why couldn't Janee stay with your sister Pam?" She rushed on before he could dismiss her suggestion. "I know we've talked about it and you don't think it would work. But maybe we're wrong. Since she and Benny don't have any children, maybe they would—"

Doug grunted and fixed his gaze on the fireplace across the room. After a moment he cleared his throat and said accusingly, "You know why Janee is with us and not with Pam."

"Because Nancy wanted it that way," Barbara replied simply.

"Because if anything ever happened to them, Nancy wanted Janee in a Christian home. On her deathbed she asked us to take Janee, Barb. You heard her. You said 'okay.' On her deathbed she asked us, for crying out loud. That's why Janee's here. That's why she's staying."

"But Pam and Benny—"

"Pam and Benny would never take Janee to church," Doug countered, his voice rising precariously. "They have no interest in God. They don't have room in their lives for Janee. They don't have room for anyone but themselves."

Barbara sat forward stiffly. She clasped her clammy hands together so that the bones of her knuckles stood out pearl-white under the thin flesh of her fingers. She wanted to shout back, *You should talk, Doug. You don't have room in your life for me anymore, nor for Janee. You're hardly ever here, and even when you are here, the real you is locked away.*

But this wasn't the time to rehash old, unresolved miseries. She needed her husband in her corner now, supporting her. "Doug," she said, the words painfully tight in her throat, "what you've got to understand is that I'm no good for Janee, either. I can't reach her. She's unhappy here. She's suffered so much already, I don't want to cause her any more hurt. Don't you see?"

Doug stood up and walked across the room. He put his hand on the fireplace mantel and leaned heavily, as if he were not sure his legs would support his bulk. His dark brows crouched over dusky, solemn, deep azure eyes. Quietly, so that Barbara had to strain to hear, he said, "I believe God wants Janee here, Barbie. You pray and search your heart. You pray for God to show you what's right. Give it some time. A few more days. Let's say a week. Next Tuesday, okay? Then, if you still think we should contact Pam, we'll talk to her and see what she has to say."

Barbara went to her husband and received his embrace, but somehow his strong arms offered little consolation. Twinges of guilt pricked at her heart. What would Doug say if he knew she had already phoned Pam and was waiting even now for her answer?

"I don't want to send Janee away," Doug said as he absently nuzzled the top of her head with his chin. "But you're my wife, Barbie. I love you. I have to consider you first."

Later that evening, as Barbara thought about the one-week deadline, she realized that setting a specific period of time for their decision about Janee gave her a curious sense of relief. She was no longer facing an interminable road with the child. If things didn't get better in the next week, and if Doug's sister cooperated, Janee could stay with Pam and Benny.

Then everything would be as it had been. Not perfect, but tolerable. Almost tolerable. Barbara would be alone again with her cherished memories of Caitlin. She and Doug still wouldn't be close, of course. They would remain polite strangers in their own home, coming and going without quite touching, careful never to scratch the surface of their emotions.

But perhaps it was better that way. Once one's emotions were unleashed, old wounds had a way of becoming raw again. Doug must have sensed that. That's why he had withdrawn after Caitlin's death, shutting down emotionally until there were no feelings left to share.

And hadn't she done the same thing in her own way? Hadn't she buried her emotions so deep that only a vague numbness remained? A torpor? A paralysis of the spirit that was better than the pain?

That is, until Janee had burst into their lives, upsetting the emotional applecart and throwing their quiet, predictable lives into chaos.

But, God willing, next Tuesday circumstances would improve dramatically for both Barbara and Janee.

Chapter Eight

Doug was home on time for dinner on Monday evening. It was a quiet, uneventful meal except for Janee slurping her spaghetti strands and Tabby meowing under the table, begging for tidbits of meatball that Janee "secretly" fed her. Barbara said nothing about the decision she and Doug would make about Janee tomorrow.

The evening passed slowly, the hours marked by an unsettling solitude. It was as if the entire earth were still, hushed, waiting. Or maybe the uneasy silence meant Doug was reflecting on the seriousness of their decision about Janee. Barbara knew he didn't agree with her, but maybe he was even more opposed than she had suspected. Would he insist that Janee stay, after all?

Janee sat quietly coloring with large wax crayons in a Donald Duck coloring book, looking the picture of innocence. Doug wasn't home often enough to see how things really were. He had no idea how painful a child's anger and animosity could be.

"Time for bed, Janee," Barbara said at last.

Janee kept her gaze fixed on her coloring book. "I don't want to."

"It's time, Janee. Run along and get into your pajamas, and I'll be up in a minute."

Janee shook her head.

"Come on, Janee," Doug broke in pleasantly. "Be a good girl for your Uncle Doug."

Reluctantly Janee left her coloring book on the sofa and trudged toward the stairs, her head lowered.

Some minutes later Barbara followed her upstairs and quietly entered the small bedroom, expecting to see a pajama-clad Janee snugly under her covers. Instead, Janee sat crouched in a corner, her gaze reproachful. Still dressed in her dungarees and pull-over shirt, she clutched her careworn bear Zowie and her Raggedy Ann doll in her arms. The bear's frayed head hung limp and the stuffed arms and legs of the cloth doll stuck out crazily in all directions. The orange yarn hair was askew, and the painted face seemed to grin mockingly at Barbara.

She forced her voice to remain calm. "I thought I told you to get ready for bed, Janee."

Janee rubbed her cheek against Raggedy Ann's ropy head. "I'm not sleepy."

"But you will be in the morning. Come on, honey. Let's go. Do as I say."

Janee jutted out her lower lip. "I don't have to. You're not my mommy!"

Barbara's cool composure evaporated. "No, I'm not your mommy, but you still must do as I say." Swiftly she crossed the room, picked up the child and put her in bed fully clothed. She placed the doll on one side of her and the bear on the other, then tucked in the blankets with quick, efficient movements. Without another word she walked out of the room, flicking off the light switch with a decisiveness that left her trembling.

Later, in her own room, lying in bed next to her slumbering husband, Barbara prayed silently, *Dear God, what else can I do with Janee? She doesn't listen to me. She defies me at every turn. I have nothing more to give.*

What about love? her conscience prodded.

It was much easier to love people en masse—the homeless, the brave, the downtrodden, all the people of the world whom one could clump together and tie with labels. But to love a person on an intimate, one-to-one basis was something else, an ability that seemed to elude Barbara completely these days.

"How do you love a child who doesn't invite love? How do you love her?" she whispered, but her voice drifted off like a fine wisp of smoke in the night, and her thoughts were muffled at last by sleep.

Early Tuesday morning, while it was still dark, Barbara felt herself jerked violently out of bed. One moment she had felt Doug's warm shoulder and torso against her back. The next moment she found herself sitting sprawled on the carpeted floor beside the bed. A deafening noise enveloped the room—the sound of a freight train rumbling through the house, its vibration rattling the walls.

Barbara stumbled blindly to her feet, then fell on her knees as the floor moved beneath her. She reached out desperately and clutched the downy comforter from her bed. She dragged it with her as the floor rippled and threw her against the massive bureau. A shooting drawer grazed her arm and spilled its contents on the floor. She scrambled out of the way as another drawer shot out and crashed against the bed. All around her the walls creaked and groaned and the windows rattled in their frames.

"Doug!" She clasped the headboard desperately, her eyes frantically searching the darkness.

"Over here." He was across the room, swallowed by shadows.

Glass shattered somewhere, followed by several loud crashes downstairs. Barbara held on tight. The floorboards beneath the carpet convulsed with quick, spasmodic jerks. The unseen ghost train rumbled through their room with a thunderous, guttural roar.

"Earthquake!" Doug yelled, his voice harsh. "Get in the hallway, Barb. In the doorway."

"I can't," she gasped.

Crashes echoed from another room—surely more drawers careening out of dressers; then another horrifying noise downstairs, and another. Barbara could imagine it: knickknacks sliding off tables, a lamp falling somewhere, paintings rattling against walls, books cascading off shelves.

"Doug!" she rasped again, but her voice was swallowed up as she was by the jarring motion—the writhing of the splintered floor beneath her feet and the unearthly groan of plaster walls stretched beyond their limits.

After a moment, the convulsive jolts subsided to a smooth rocking motion. From deep within the house came low doleful moanings, as if its very timbers had ruptured.

The temblor seemed eternal—waves of an ocean going on and on, pervasive, ubiquitous. But gradually—actually within moments—the tremors ceased and the house was still again, except for Tabby's woeful mewl somewhere downstairs.

Barbara released the bedpost and straightened her body. Her muscles ached; she felt stiff. And yet she was trembling profoundly, every muscle of her body as weak and pliant as shifting sand.

"Stay where you are," warned Doug. "There's glass everywhere."

"You be careful, too."

Her eyes were accustomed to the dark now. She could see Doug's robust frame as he negotiated his way around the debris. "Barbara, are you okay?" He gathered her into his strong arms and held her close.

"I think so. Nothing hurts, except my fingers from holding so tightly to the bed."

"Thank God!"

She pressed her cheek against Doug's muscled chest, its warmth reassuring, and marveled that everything had happened and was over in a minute. She couldn't comprehend it. A minute—and yet forever had passed through that minute, absorbed it, absorbed everything, her strength, her senses. Her thoughts were out of focus, blurred. She couldn't think.

And then, abruptly, with a chilled shudder, she remembered Janee.

"Janee! What about Janee?" she demanded.

Doug looked at her blankly for a moment, his face masked in shadows, then exclaimed, "Great Scott! The poor kid's all alone!"

"We've got to get to her, Doug." The words wrenched from Barbara's lips. "Now! She could be hurt. Terrified."

Doug restrained her. "Wait, Barb. Put on your slippers. I'll find a flashlight. We don't know what we're going to find."

"I'll turn on the light," she said, flipping the wall switch. "Nothing," she sighed. "The power must be out."

"With that terrible jolt the whole Los Angeles basin could be without power. Man, if this wasn't the quake's epicenter, someplace else around here must be in a heap of rubble by now."

Barbara felt for her terry-cloth robe and pulled it around her shoulders, but the cold in her bones had nothing to do with the temperature. She could smell the dankness of must and plaster dust seeping from the fractured innards of the house. "There could be another quake on its heels, Doug. A bigger one."

"Let's get to Janee."

Gingerly he pushed the clutter aside—piles of clothing, a toppled lamp, an overturned end table. Barbara was almost glad it was dark so that she didn't have to see all the destruction. Doug took her hand and led her through the wreckage and down the hallway to Janee's room. The first rays of dawn trickled through the shattered skylight overhead.

"Janee!" Doug called as he reached for her doorknob. He tried the door but it wouldn't open. He gave it a shove. "Something's blocking the door." He tried again, and this time the door gave.

Barbara followed Doug inside, her eyes fixed on the moving circle of light as he panned the dusky room, surveying the damage. Toys and clothes were strewn everywhere. But Janee's bed was empty.

Barbara's throat constricted. "Janee!"

The bright oval of light fell on a tiny figure standing at the far wall, pressed fiercely against it. Janee's sea-green eyes were round as saucers and vivid with alarm. She looked unreal somehow, the gesture of her tiny body seemingly frozen in a moment of time, as if she were a delicate piece of sculpture, not quite complete and terribly vulnerable.

On the floor lay her Raggedy Ann and Zowie, crumpled beneath the spilled-out contents of a dresser drawer. Toys had fallen off the shelf—dolls, games, books.

Barbara took a tentative step. "Are you all right, honey?"

The child began to scream.

Barbara made her way through the rubble and gathered Janee into her arms. She kissed the tears, the mussed hair, and felt the warmth and anguish of Janee's small frantic body. In that moment, as the child's anguish became her own, Barbara pleaded, "Don't cry, Janee. We're here, honey. It's going to be okay."

Something stirred inside Barbara as she held the trembling youngster close. "Don't be scared," she whispered into Janee's hair as she muffled the child's sobs against her breast. "We're right here for you, honey."

"Is she okay, Barb?"

"I think so. You're the doctor. You check."

Doug reached over and lifted Janee into his arms. "Hey, sweetie, let's go downstairs and find Tabby, okay? Then we'll go outside and watch the sun come up." He looked back at Barbara. "I've got to turn off the gas. The pipes may be broken."

She covered her mouth in alarm. "We don't need a fire on top of all this."

Doug led the way downstairs, one step after another. The crystal chandelier still swung languidly in the foyer. In the living room gray ribbons of light streamed through shattered windows, revealing the scope of the damage. Barbara's beloved piano was overturned and the wall-to-wall bookcases had spewed out all their contents. Her elegant furniture had been transformed into piles of pick-up sticks.

Nausea clenched Barbara's stomach. "Oh, Doug," she groaned.

"Don't look, Barb. Let's just find Tabby and get outside. I don't want to be in here if another temblor hits."

"Tabby!" Barbara called. "Here, Tabby! Where are you?"

A faint mewling came from the dining room. Doug handed Janee to Barbara. "You two go outside. I'll be right out."

"Be careful, Doug."

He squeezed her hand and urged her on. "Looks like the foyer is open. But be careful on the porch. And watch out for downed power lines in the grass."

Barbara carried Janee outside, dodging chunks of stucco and concrete on the porch. She padded through the moist grass until she found a safe place to sit. Thank goodness, no high-tension wires nearby. She stooped down, holding a shivering Janee close. The dewy grass was cold on Barbara's bare legs and the ground felt hard after the cozy warmth of her bed. She pulled part of her robe over

Janee's thin cotton pajamas. "Is that better, honey?"

Janee nodded. "Wh-where's Tabby?"

"Uncle Doug is getting her. She'll be right here."

Janee heaved a sigh. "I don't want her to die."

"Oh, Tabby will be fine," Barbara assured her, too brightly. "You know what they say about cats. They have nine lives."

"What does that mean?"

"It means...Tabby will be fine." *Please, God, make it so!* As Barbara looked up and down the street, the full import of what had happened struck her. People stood in their front yards in nervous little clusters. Babies cried. Streetlights and telephone poles stood at precarious angles. Crackling high wires drooped near the ground. A two-story home four doors away was in flames. Sirens wailed in the distance, surely echoing the laments that rose from stunned survivors across the shaken city.

Within minutes Doug emerged from the house with Tabby. It was an odd sight—her husband descending the porch steps in his pajama bottoms and cradling a terrified cat against his brawny chest. Doug approached and bent down, allowing the jittery feline to jump from his arms into Janee's. "Be careful," he warned her. "Tabby's scared, so hold her very gently. Smooth her fur and tell her she doesn't have to be afraid."

Janee's small arms circled the fat, bristly-haired cat. "It's okay, Tabby," she crooned, patting

Tabby's head. "You aren't hurt. See? Uncle Doug saved you."

Doug sat down on the ground beside Barbara. "I turned off the gas. Thank God, I didn't see any sign of fire."

"What now?"

"I don't know. It looks like all our neighbors are wondering the same thing."

"Is the house as bad as it looks?" Barbara's voice caught. "Can we salvage anything?"

Doug sat forward, his head lowered, his elbows on his knees. "I don't know, Barb. I sure hope so."

"What about the house itself? It'll be all right, won't it?"

Doug made a gravelly sound low in his throat. "I looked around a little. Saw some major cracks in the walls. I hope it's just surface damage that some paint and drywall can repair. It'll take a structural engineer to determine if the house is livable."

A shiver of comprehension swept over Barbara. "You mean, we could lose the entire house? They might have to tear it down?"

"It depends on how much damage it sustained. I pray to God it can be repaired. But meanwhile..."

"Where will we stay?"

"I don't know. A hotel?"

"If everyone around us has this kind of damage, the hotels will be overflowing by evening."

Doug reached over and clasped Barbara's hand. "I don't want you staying here in town, anyway."

"Not stay in town? What do you mean?"

"The aftershocks. They could be as bad as the original quake. Or worse. They could finish what the first one started."

Barbara shrugged helplessly. Tears welled in her eyes. The hopelessness and severity of the situation was dawning on her. "Then where can we go? What can we do?"

"If there was only somewhere to go, away from the quake area." He paused for a long moment, then exclaimed, "Of course, why didn't I think of it sooner? The cabin!"

She looked at him. "The cabin? You mean our cabin at Lake Arrowhead?"

"Why not. It's far enough away that it shouldn't experience any serious jolts from this quake."

"You mean we'll just get in the car and drive to the mountains...now?"

"Why not? What can we do here? I'll turn everything off and lock up the house, and we'll go. Of course, it may not be as easy as we think. The freeways could be damaged. Traffic could be backed up for miles."

Barbara hesitated. "But shouldn't someone stay here to keep an eye on the house."

"Someone will." Doug squeezed her shoulder, as if silently asking her to understand. "I'll drive you to Lake Arrowhead, Barbie, then I'm coming back."

"Here?"

"Yes, here. I'm a doctor. I'm going to be needed in the next few days."

Barbara stared hard at him. "Then I'm not leaving, either. Why should I go without you? We can both help where we're needed."

"Barb, I really—"

The ground began to shake again. Barbara clutched Janee, and Doug wrapped his arms around both of them. "Hold on," he directed. "It's an aftershock."

Barbara could feel the strange tug and pull of the earth, as if some sleepy underground giant were rousing himself. Janee screamed, and Tabby bristled like a porcupine and would have leapt from Janee's arms if Doug hadn't seized the nape of her neck. A crash resounded from the neighbor's yard; their brick chimney had toppled like a child's plastic blocks.

After a few moments the quaking subsided; the sleeping giant was still.

"See what I mean, Barb?" said Doug. "It's not safe here. You've got to let me take you to the mountains."

"If it's not safe here for us, it's not safe for you, either," Barbara argued. "Stay with us, Doug. Please!"

He ran his fingers through her sleep-tousled hair. "I can't, Barbie. I've got to do what I can here." He stood up and brushed off his knees. "Now you and Janee and Tabby go get in the car. Turn on the radio. They should have some news about the quake—magnitude, epicenter. It had to be at least an eight."

"Wait, Doug. Where are you going?"

"Inside. For my wallet. And some clothes and blankets."

"Get my purse if you can find it. But be careful!"

As Doug disappeared inside, Barbara gazed around her broken, once-beautiful neighborhood in disbelief. Dawn had washed the horizon with brilliant splashes of orange and pink that illuminated the surrounding houses and streets. The golden rays of morning underscored the scope of the quake's damage, and what Barbara saw made her weep.

Chapter Nine

"Well, ladies and gentlemen, as you all know, sunny Southern California awoke this morning to a huge seismic jolt. The magnitude was eight point one, according to the Richter scale. The quake was felt as far north as San Francisco and as far east as Phoenix. Several heart-pounding aftershocks have rocked the Southland since the original temblor at 5:38 this morning. The epicenter is believed to be about two miles east of Pasadena. Large sections of Glendale and Pasadena are without power, and numerous fires have been reported. Reports of injuries are coming in. Several overpasses have been severely damaged and most freeways are bumper-to-bumper traffic. If you're trying to get out of town this morning, you might as well sit back and relax. You have a long wait ahead of you."

"That's for sure," said Doug, switching off the

radio and white-knuckle gripping the steering wheel. Irritation was thick in his voice. They were creeping along on the 210 freeway and were still no farther than Monrovia. "At this rate we'll get to Lake Arrowhead by next Tuesday."

"At least we're all in the same boat," said Barbara.

Doug cast a quick glance into the back seat where Janee lay sleeping with Tabby in her arms. "The thing is, Barb, I was hoping to get you and Janee settled in the cabin this afternoon so I could get back in town by tonight."

"So soon? I was hoping you'd stay with us a day or two. If you come back, where will you stay?"

"The hospital. With all the injuries, it'll be a madhouse. I may be working day and night. So I'll catch a few winks on the sofa in my office."

"How do you feel about treating patients again?"

Doug was silent for a moment. "I'll do what I have to do. Serve where I'm needed."

Barbara twisted her purse strap. "And our house—what about our house?"

"I'll try to get someone on it as soon as I can. The housing authorities will be backed up with demands. People wanting to know if their homes are safe to occupy. Meanwhile, I'll go back inside in the daylight and see what I can save."

"The refrigerator needs to be emptied out. With the power off, everything will rot."

"I'll see what I can do."

"But be careful, Doug. I don't want you getting hurt."

He reached over and patted her hand. "I'll be fine."

Barbara stifled a sob. "I can't believe this is happening. Our home. Our beautiful home. We've worked so many years for it. Now it's in shambles."

"Don't think about it, Barb. Just be thankful we all made it out alive, without a scratch. That's something to be thankful for."

She nodded. "I know it is, and I'm trying to be thankful. It's just that I never dreamed we would ever be...homeless!"

"It may not be that bad, hon. A little cleanup, some paint and plaster, and the place could be as good as new."

"I pray to God you're right."

They drove in silence for a long time, inching along until they reached the 57 freeway. Traffic finally opened up, allowing Doug to accelerate to the speed limit, and was lighter still when they turned onto the San Bernardino freeway heading for Lake Arrowhead.

By the time they had driven through scenic, majestic Rim Forest and were approaching the quaint mountain town of Blue Jay, Barbara began to feel a twinge of nostalgia. "Goodness, this brings back memories," she sighed. "When were we last here?"

Doug's voice was tight. "Don't you remember? Caitlin's last summer."

Barbara felt her breath catch in her chest, as if she'd been struck. "Yes, I remember. She had so much fun swimming in the lake and going hiking with you."

"Remember the day we drove over to Santa's Village and she got to see Santa's workshop and all the elves? She was so excited, you'd think she'd died and gone to heaven." Doug's voice broke off and a tendon tightened in his jaw. He looked over at Barbara, his face blanched white. "I'm sorry, hon. That was a stupid thing to say. I don't know how I could—"

"It's okay, Doug."

"It was just a crazy expression."

"I know. But it's the truth. Caitlin is in heaven."

Doug drummed his fingers on the steering wheel. "Look, Barb, we're passing the Blue Jay Ice Castle."

She followed his gaze out the side window. "Isn't that the skating rink where some of the Olympic skaters practice?"

"Yeah. Especially that one gold medalist. I can't think of her name. She used to practice here all the time." He turned onto the narrow, winding road heading for Lake Arrowhead Village. The picturesque road was lined with towering pines and giant cedars. Doug rolled down the window and inhaled deeply. "Man, smell that fresh mountain air. No smog. Just a clean, sweet breeze. I'll tell you, Barb, this place brings back lots of memories."

"Same here," she conceded in a small voice.

"Remember the night we met?"

"How could I forget? The Cottage Restaurant on Highway 18."

"Best Italian food on the mountain. You were there with that guy—the mountain man."

"You always called him that. His name was Trent. Trent Townsend. A very nice man."

"I never trusted him. Something in his eyes and his manner. Like he didn't care what impression he made on people. A real wildlife freak. I think he preferred bears and squirrels to people."

"Really, Doug, you're faulting him for loving animals?"

"No, it's just... He always dressed like a lumberjack. Like he thought he was Paul Bunyan or something."

"He did not. He was wearing a suit when you met him."

"Oh, you remember?"

"Of course I remember. It was my eighteenth birthday. Trent took me out to celebrate."

"And, as I recall, the two of you looked like you were having a pretty good time."

"We were. I cared for Trent, you know that."

"And he was madly in love with you."

"That's how you saw it. Our families were neighbors on the mountain. We spent every summer together from the time we were toddlers."

"And you probably would have married him if I hadn't come along that night."

Barbara rolled her eyes. "You should talk. You were there with my girlfriend Sheila."

Doug chuckled. "Sheila. Now there was a girl!"

Barbara scowled. "She was a little on the wild side, as I recall."

Doug's voice took on a gently teasing tone. "Yes, she was something of a spitfire. Not a girl you soon forget."

"How the four of us ended up spending the evening together, I'll never know," said Barbara.

Doug's hand dropped from the steering wheel to Barbara's knee, which he squeezed fondly. "You don't know? It was my doing. The moment I met you I thought, I've got to know her better. I suggested we make it a foursome."

"And while Sheila was in the rest room and Trent was paying the bill, you asked for my phone number."

"And the rest is history, as they say," said Doug with a seductive smile. "Although I don't think Trent ever forgave me for stealing his girl."

"He must have. He married Sheila, didn't he?"

"I suppose he considered it the ultimate revenge. I stole his girl, so he stole mine." Doug glanced over at Barbara and winked. "But I got the best deal."

Barbara laughed. How good it felt to laugh. When

was the last time she and Doug had reminisced like this? And laughed together!

"Almost there," he said as he took another winding turn through the giant pines. "We'll stop by the Village and pick up some groceries and supplies, then head for the cabin."

"What about electricity?"

"You'll have to call the power company tomorrow. And the phone company."

"I have my cell phone. And those kerosene lamps in the pantry will do for tonight."

"You'll be roughing it for a few days in the cabin, Barb, but it should be better than sitting in some hotel room waiting for the next aftershock."

"You're right," she agreed. "It's just..."

"I know. It's not home."

"I guess that's it. The cabin belonged to my parents. Every summer I had to leave my friends and go live in the cabin with my folks. They loved the mountains, the quaint towns, the rustic environment, the so-called untouched wilderness. But I longed for my friends and the city with all its hustle and bustle, not to mention the luxuries and comforts of home."

"It won't be forever, Barb. Maybe I can get the house fixed and livable again in a few weeks."

"And if you believe that, you might as well believe in the tooth fairy. It could take months, Doug, what with the red tape of insurance claims and building permits. And with all the damaged homes, construction workers will be in short supply. And that's assuming our house can be salvaged."

"We'll just have to take it a day at a time, Barb."

"I know, Doug. I'll try."

They were at Lake Arrowhead Village now, an elegant shopping area with red-roofed, brown-trimmed buildings that exuded a quaint, Old World charm. Its picturesque alpine shops and restaurants could have been plucked from the heart of Europe. Doug pulled into a parking space near the clock tower and remained in the car with Janee and Tabby, while Barbara went inside and purchased the necessary toiletries and supplies. Thank goodness, the cabin already contained some things, such as dishes, silverware and bedding, Barbara thought. But what about laundry detergent and dishwashing liquid?

And food. There would be nothing in the cabin. She would need to get all the staples, plus ice to keep things cold until the refrigerator could be turned on. And the electric stove. How could she cook without a stove? She would have to buy bread and canned tuna and lots of peanut butter and jelly for Janee.

The shopping trip took a half hour, plus another hour for a stop at a fast-food restaurant, and then they were back on the road, heading south toward Rainbow Drive. It was late afternoon when they pulled up beside the knotty pine, A-frame chalet nestled in a verdant alcove of the lush woodland.

"Looks the same outside," said Doug as he unlocked the door. "The caretaker's kept the place up." He pushed open the door and stepped back with a little flourish, letting Barbara and Janee enter. Janee, carrying Tabby snugly in her arms, looked around and asked uncertainly, "Where are we?"

"This is going to be our home for a while," said Barbara with forced enthusiasm. "Sort of like a vacation."

A vacation? Who was she kidding? The place was filthy with dust and dreary. Gauzy cobwebs drooped from the high-beamed ceiling to the cedar tongue-and-groove flooring. Barbara's gaze moved from the open-hearth stone fireplace to the wall of leaded-glass windows. "The place needs a lot of elbow grease, no doubt about it."

Doug drew a sharp breath. "Man alive, I didn't know it would be so bad inside."

Barbara shook her head. "No caretakers in here."

"We could go to a bed-and-breakfast tonight, and clean the place tomorrow."

"No, Doug. Everything will be filled up by this time of day. I'll clean the bedroom and make the beds so we can get some sleep." She gave him a second glance. "You are staying tonight, aren't you?"

He nodded. "It'll be dark soon. I'll head back to town in the morning."

She expelled a sigh of relief. "Good. I don't think I could handle this place tonight by myself."

Chapter Ten

Early the next morning Barbara and Doug tackled the cleanup of the cabin, Barbara dusting and polishing furniture and cleaning the kitchen, Doug mopping floors and scrubbing windows. He kept one ear tuned to his battery-operated radio for the latest updates on the quake damage.

"Six dead so far," he told Barbara as he carried the mop pail to the back door. "Hundreds injured. I phoned the hospital. They can use all the medical help they can get."

"So you'll be leaving," she said, more an acknowledgment than a question.

"Right. I don't feel I have any choice." He touched her chin lightly, as if somehow seeking her approval. "Will you and Janee be all right here alone?"

She nodded. "We'll be roughing it for a few days until the utilities are turned on."

"At least there's water."

"Right. Thank God for small favors."

"I know you'll feel lost without a car."

Barbara put her fingers to her lips. "I hadn't thought of that. I really am stuck here, aren't I?"

"When things simmer down at the hospital, I'll get one of the guys to come up with me. I'll drive your car and ride back with him."

"You make it sound like we're going to be here a long time."

"I don't know, Barb. We just have to be prepared for...whatever comes." He jingled his car keys in his hand. "I'd better go. Give Janee a kiss goodbye for me when she wakes up."

"She was so tired last night, she may sleep till noon."

"Let her. It'll give you some time to make your phone calls."

Barbara walked Doug outside to their automobile. The air was clean, invigorating, and fragrant with the scent of pine. The late September breeze wafted over her, surprisingly gentle and warm. Maybe spending a few days in the mountains wouldn't be so bad, after all.

Doug leaned over and kissed her lips. "Take care, hon. Keep your cell phone nearby. I'll call and check on you later today."

She straightened his collar. "It'll seem strange..."

"What will?"

"Sleeping without you beside me tonight. It's been ages since we were apart overnight."

"You're right. Not since my intern days." He climbed into his car and gave a little salute.

She waved back and watched as he backed out of the narrow drive. She didn't move until he was out of sight.

A hollow feeling settled in her chest as she walked back inside the cabin, a peculiar sensation that there was more she wanted to say to Doug before he drove away, an odd impulse to call him back and rush into his arms and tell him...tell him what? She didn't know.

Barbara had just finished phoning the utility companies when she heard Janee stirring. Janee emerged from the bedroom, a sad-faced little waif, whimpering and rubbing her eyes with her fists. Barbara went to her and smoothed back her tousled curls. "What's the matter, honey? A bad dream?"

Janee nodded. "A big monster was chasing me. He was shaking the house, trying to make me come out. I was scared."

Barbara took her hand and led her to the kitchen. "There's no monster, sweetheart. I bet you were thinking about the earthquake. I've thought about it, too. It was scary, wasn't it?"

Janee looked up wide-eyed. "You were scared, too?"

Barbara took a carton of milk from the ice chest on the counter. "Sure. Everyone gets scared sometime. But we got through it, and we're just fine, aren't we?"

"I guess so," Janee said without conviction.

"And you know what? Here in our cabin on the mountain, we won't feel any more earthquakes, because they're far away from us now."

It took a minute for Barbara's words to process themselves in Janee's mind. Suddenly she grinned and said, "I'm hungry."

Barbara reached into a grocery sack. "I figured you would be. That's why I've got your favorite cereal right here." She held up a bright-colored box of sugarcoated oats.

Janee clapped her hands. "My favorite! Crispy Creatures!"

Barbara smiled. "And not a monster among them!" She got Janee settled with her cereal at the small drop-leaf table, then returned to her chores.

Already the cabin was beginning to gleam. Now if she just had some fresh flowers for the window box and some new café curtains. Even without the frills, it wasn't a bad place to hang your hat for a few days. Not like the luxury of home, of course, but with a little sprucing up the cabin would be comfortable and pleasant. And filled with memories of her parents and her youth. Maybe too many memories. But she wouldn't allow herself to dwell on the past. The past always had a way of betraying the present and stealing joy and hope from the future. No, the past would remain...in the past.

"Aunt Barbara?" It was Janee, tugging on her shirttail. "I'm finished eating. Can I watch TV?"

Barbara was about to say "sure," when she remembered they wouldn't have electricity for another day or two. "I'm sorry, honey. You'll have to think of something else to do."

Janee looked around. "Where are all my toys?"

Whoops! Barbara hadn't thought about toys. How was she going to keep this child entertained without toys or TV? Suddenly, she had an idea. "Janee, let's go outside." She took Janee's hand and led her out the back door and down the rough-hewn steps where the entire forest was their backyard. There had to be something to do here, she thought. Pick wildflowers. Collect colorful stones. Watch squirrels. "Isn't it beautiful, Janee? All the big trees and flowers and rocks? Do you want to go for a walk?"

"Will we see little animals?"

"Maybe. Keep watching, okay?"

A fat brown squirrel scampered by and darted up a tree.

"There's one!" Janee squealed, breaking free and scampering after the animal.

"No, Janee, come here! Don't touch!"

Janee trudged back. "I want to keep the little squirrel."

"You can't, honey. It belongs here in the wilds. It probably has a little family nearby. He's probably collecting acorns for food."

"What are acorns?"

Barbara stooped down and picked one up. "See, it's like a little nut and it comes from the big oak tree. The squirrels gather them and take them home for dinner."

"Can we eat them, too?"

"No, honey, just the squirrels."

Barbara heard a rustling sound behind her and then a booming male voice. A voice from the past. "Hey, Barb, is that you?"

She whirled around, a smile breaking on her lips. "Trent! Trent Townsend. I can't believe it. Is that really you?"

Trent came striding across the wide expanse of grass—a tall, ruggedly handsome man with sturdy, tanned features and curly, flyaway brown hair brushed loosely over his forehead. He was wearing a flannel shirt, jeans and cowboy boots. "If you aren't a sight for sore eyes, darlin'!" He pulled her into his arms before she could utter a word. He wore the same spicy aftershave she remembered from their courting days. "What are you doing up here on the mountain, Barb, honey? A vacation?"

She stepped back and pushed her own wind-tossed curls away from her face. She covered her eyes to block out the noonday sun, suddenly wishing she'd put on a little makeup. "Not a vacation exactly. More like trying to get away from all the aftershocks.''

He grinned, showing white teeth and warm, crinkly eyes. ''That was quite a jolt the other day. We felt it here, but it was just a sweet little rocking motion. It woke me up, then nearly put me back to sleep.''

''Well, it nearly wrecked our house,'' said Barbara.

''You're kidding, darlin'.''

''I wish I were. Doug insisted I come up here until things settle down in the city.''

''How is Doug?''

''Fine. Busy as ever.''

Trent nodded toward Janee. ''Yours?''

Barbara's face flushed. ''No. Doug's sister's girl.''

''But you have a daughter, right? Didn't I hear that?''

''Uh, yes, I did.'' Barbara's mouth went dry. ''It's a long story, Trent. I—''

''It's okay. I have a few of those myself. Long stories, I mean.''

She looked over at the log cabin next door. ''Are you vacationing?''

He rubbed his forehead, as if weighing his answer. ''No, Barb, I'm settled here for good.''

''You're living here on the mountain?''

He nodded. ''Been here nearly a year.''

Barbara shifted from one foot to the other. It felt

strange making idle conversation with a man she had once loved. "I've forgotten, Trent. Do you and Sheila have children?"

He kicked at a clump of earth with his leather boot. "No, darlin'. We didn't have kids. Wish we had."

She looked at him curiously. Darkness clouded his gray-green eyes. Something was wrong. One of those long stories he didn't want to talk about? "Is it Sheila?" she asked gently. "Are you two divorced?"

"Naw. Nothing like that."

His voice took on a heaviness that stirred a sense of foreboding inside her. "What is it, Trent?"

He looked her square in the eyes and said, "Sheila died. An accident. Last year."

"Trent, I'm so sorry. I hadn't heard," Barbara said quietly.

He shrugged. "I wasn't too good about letting folks know. I should have called or written, but she was the one who always kept in touch. You know me. A loner. I didn't want to talk to anyone."

"I know the feeling," Barbara admitted. "Doug and I...we lost our daughter four years ago." She hadn't planned to mention Caitlin, but now it seemed the proper thing to do. In a way, she and Trent were comrades in grief.

"Four years ago," he echoed solemnly.

"But it feels like yesterday."

"I know what you mean. Just when I think I'm

starting to pull myself together, something happens, and I feel like I'm back at square one again."

"That's perfectly normal," Barbara assured him with an ironic smile. "I should know."

Trent swung his arm around her shoulder, a comforting, protective gesture. "Looks like we've got a lot of catching up to do. Why don't you come on over for some coffee and chitchat."

"I don't know, Trent..."

"Come on, Barb. One cup. Decaffeinated, right? And ten minutes of your time. For old times' sake. You always were great at picking up my spirits."

She eased away from his touch. "Maybe one of these days, Trent. I'm not much for socializing right now."

"Sure, I gotcha." He gazed around, squinting against the sunlight. "Listen, you need any help settling in? How about firewood? You got firewood? It's autumn and we'll be having some cold nights up here."

"I...I don't know if we have firewood or not. We just drove up yesterday, and I'm still—"

"Sure, I understand. I have plenty of wood. I'll bring some over." He looked toward the driveway. "Do you have a car?"

"It's back home. Doug drove me up. He'll be back in a few days. Maybe even sooner."

"Well, if you need a ride to the Village or anywhere else, you just say the word. I'll give you a lift wherever you need to go."

"Thanks, Trent, but I couldn't impose."

He stepped closer and gently knuckled her chin. "Sure, you can. What are old friends for?"

Barbara was almost relieved when Janee came running up with a fistful of wildflowers. "Look, Aunt Barbara! Pretty flowers!"

"Goodness, they're lovely. Let's get them into water."

Janee held out her other hand. "Look what else I got. A funny shell."

Barbara chuckled at the brown object in Janee's palm. "That's not a shell, honey. That's a pinecone. It came from the big pine tree."

"What's it for?"

"Well, when I was a little girl, I made dolls out of pinecones."

Janee jumped up and down. "Make me a doll, please, Aunt Barbara!"

Barbara looked over at Trent and shrugged. "I'd better take a rain check on that coffee. I have some serious doll-making to do here."

Trent grinned and took a couple of steps backward, his thumbs hooked on his jeans' pockets. "Looks that way. But you haven't seen the last of me, darlin'. Our paths will cross again, and that's a promise."

Barbara gave Trent a parting wave, then took Janee's hand firmly in hers. "Come on, honey. Get that old basket by the porch. If we're going to make dolls, we have to find ourselves some more pinecones. And maybe a few acorns, too.''

Fifteen minutes later, the two trooped up the back porch steps with a hefty basket of pinecones and their pockets bulging with acorns. Janee was ecstatic. They went inside, and Barbara set the basket on the kitchen table, then went in search of scissors, glue, poster paints and scraps of colorful material. She spread the items out on the table, then sat down across from Janee. ''See how we make funny little people? Here's the head and here's the body.'' She glued an acorn to the top of a pinecone, then added a scrap of red flannel for a coat and painted a happy face on the acorn.

Janee clapped her hands in glee. ''Let me do it!''

During the next two hours Barbara helped Janee make an entire family of pinecones—a mommy and daddy, three children, and a dog and cat. ''I made pinecone families just like this when I was little,'' Barbara told Janee as she put the finishing touches on the cat's face. She remembered as if it were yesterday. ''We sat right here at this very table.''

Janee looked up, wide-eyed. ''Did your mommy help you?''

''Yes, she did,'' Barbara said softly, the poignant recollections tumbling into her consciousness. ''She helped me just like I'm helping you.''

Janee selected several stout, rough-hewn little figures and arranged them in a row on the table. She pointed at each one and said with exaggerated importance, "This one is Uncle Doug and this one is Aunt Barbara. And here's Janee and Tabby. Look, we're a family!"

A surge of emotion caught Barbara by surprise. Was it possible? Could they really be a family someday?

Chapter Eleven

A strange thing happened during the crisp, autumn days Barbara spent with Janee on the mountain. As the two hiked and played games and popped corn in the fireplace and watched sunsets together and counted stars, they became friends of sorts. Barbara couldn't believe what was happening. As impossible as it seemed, she and Janee were having fun together.

Perhaps it was because they had no other distractions. They had each other. They had no choice but to find things to entertain themselves. And yet it was more than that. It was as if the cabin had given them a fresh start, a new outlook. Gone were the old animosities, the wariness, the defensive, self-imposed walls that each had erected.

On Friday night Doug drove back up the mountain, and Barbara and Janee greeted him as if he were a long-lost traveler. "We're having hot dogs, Uncle Doug," Janee exclaimed. "We roast them on sticks in the fireplace. They taste so good."

Doug swept Janee up in his arms and planted a loud, smacking kiss on her forehead. "Is that so? I bet marshmallows taste real good over the fire, too."

"They do, Uncle Doug. We roasted lots of marshmallows. They get all black and crispy, but inside they're soft and gooey."

"I remember those, too." Doug set Janee down and reached for Barbara. "Looks like you two are having a pretty good time roughing it in the woods."

Barbara felt her face grow warm. Why was it so hard to admit to Doug how special this week had been? "We've managed quite well, thank you."

"Look at the little people we made, Uncle Doug." Janee thrust several pinecone figures into his hands.

"Well, well, what have we here?"

"It's a family, Uncle Doug. A mommy and daddy and their little girl and their cute little kitty. A family. Like us."

Doug looked at Barbara and raised one eyebrow, a curious grin playing on his lips. "Looks to me like a lot has happened since I left my two girls here in the wilderness."

Barbara brushed off his remark with a sly chuckle. "We'll talk about it later. Right now, I'd better check the chili for our hot dogs."

Later, after Janee was asleep, Barbara and Doug sat on the front porch, rocking in the creaking oak swing. The brisk air was fragrant with the sweet, piquant scents of the forest. Doug slipped his arm around Barbara and rubbed her bare arm. "Cold?"

"No. Just right."

He inhaled deeply. "This is the life, huh? Solitude. Peace and quiet. Time stands still in this place. Gives you a chance to catch your breath and clear your head."

Barbara nestled her head against his shoulder. "It was a rough week for you, wasn't it?"

"Not one of my best. Chaos at the hospital, of course, with all the quake injuries. And tons of red tape trying to get something done on the house."

"Did you find out anything?"

"Yeah, I finally got someone out there to survey the damage. They say the house is sound structurally, but it still needs a lot of work."

"Then I guess Janee and I won't be going home anytime soon."

"Afraid not, hon. Frankly, it could be months, with labor in such short supply."

Barbara looked up at him, tracing the solid line of his jaw. "I can't put my life on hold that long, Doug. You know that."

"We may have no choice—unless you want to rent a place in town. But like I said, they're in short supply these days, too. Besides, it looks like you and Janee are doing very well together here. I haven't seen the kid this happy since she came to live with us."

Barbara nodded. "It's amazing what the change of scenery has done for her. And for me, too, I suppose. I don't quite know what to make of it."

"Don't try to analyze it, Barb. Just be grateful for it."

"I am. I almost feel like my old self, whoever that is. I thought I'd be the last one to admit this, Doug, but Janee's been good for me. We've been good for each other. I don't know why it couldn't have been like this back home."

He nuzzled the top of her head. "Maybe you were afraid to let it happen, to let yourself care about a child again."

"Maybe." She gazed up at him. "Has it been that way for you, too?"

"What do you mean?" he asked warily.

"I'm not trying to start anything, Doug. I swear I'm not. But you brought it up, so I've got to say what I think. Maybe you're afraid of letting your emotions go and really loving someone because you're afraid of being hurt again. Maybe that's why you throw yourself into your work and spend so little time with us."

He shrugged, his brow furrowed. "I don't know. Maybe. But it looks to me like you and Janee have done just fine without me."

"It would have been more fun with you here."

"I'm here now, and I'll prove I'm not afraid to

let my emotions go and experience a little love." He lowered his head and kissed her on the lips, lightly, tantalizingly.

She traced the line of his lips with her fingertips. "I think you deliberately misunderstood my remark."

"Love is love, Barbie, girl. And you've got me for the whole weekend."

She slipped her hand around the back of his neck and murmured playfully, "Then we'll have to think of something exciting to do."

"You want excitement? You've got it, baby." He kissed her soundly, until she had to turn her head to catch her breath.

"Keep this up, Doug, and I'll feel like a teenager again."

He whispered against her cheek, "Remember how we used to sit on this swing in the summertime kissing until your mom came out and shooed me away?"

Barbara drew back slightly and tucked several strands of hair behind her ear. "Speaking of those days, you won't believe who's back on the mountain."

"Let me guess. Someone we both know and love?"

"Actually, he was never your favorite person."

Doug made a guffawing sound low in his throat. "Great Scott! Not old lover boy, Trent."

"How'd you guess?"

Doug sat back, his arm still around Barbara, but his ardor cooled for the moment. "What's he doing here? On vacation? I suppose his folks left him the cabin."

"Yes, they did, but he's not here on vacation."

"Don't tell me he moved here. Came with his wife, Sheila. I suppose they have a dozen kids by now."

"No. None." Barbara's voice grew solemn. Somehow it was hard to get the words out. A chill traveled up her backbone. "She died, Doug. Sheila died about a year ago. In an accident. Trent came here alone. He's grieving."

Doug released her and sat forward, resting his elbows on his knees. "Well, we know what that's like, don't we?"

"I didn't want to tell him we still haven't found our way out of that long, dark tunnel. I wanted to be positive and encouraging and tell him everything would be fine. But I couldn't think of a thing to say, except 'I'm sorry.'"

Doug sat back again and looked at Barbara with an expression she couldn't quite read. "So the guy's been over here a few times?"

"Once or twice. To say hello. To bring some kindling. That's all." She searched Doug's eyes, noticing the way the moonlight and shadows played on his face. "You're not jealous, are you?"

Doug reared back with mock indignation. "Me?

Are you kidding? Why would I be jealous? I'm the one who won. I got the girl."

She snuggled against his shoulder. "You sure did. For keeps."

"Still, with me gone so much, I don't want him coming over here and getting any bright ideas."

"For goodness' sake, what kind of ideas would he get?"

"That you're available again."

"He knows better."

"Well, I'd still keep an eye on him. I don't want him thinking he can cry on your shoulder whenever he pleases."

"Cry? Are you serious? He's like you, Doug. He doesn't cry."

"You say that like it's a fault."

"Maybe it is."

He stiffened and pulled away. "You're not going to get into that, are you?"

"Into what?"

"You know."

She looked steadily at him and finally forced out the words, "You mean the fact that I never saw you cry over Caitlin?"

"I cried."

"Once. When they told us she was gone."

"I cried other times."

"I never saw you."

"Take my word for it."

In a small voice she said, "You never cried with me."

His voice took on a hard edge. "There's no law that says I've got to blubber all over the place when something bad happens."

His words struck her like a slap. "Something bad? For crying out loud, Doug! Caitlin died!"

Doug put his head in his hands. "Do we have to get into this now, Barbara? For the first time in ages we were having a nice time. A pleasant conversation. No strings attached. No ulterior motives. No hidden agenda. Just a normal conversation like other people have."

She couldn't let go of the knot of anger tightening in her chest. "You cried when Nancy died."

"What's that got to do with anything?"

Barbara moved to her side of the swing and crossed her arms defensively. She was cold now, but she didn't want Doug to know. She was too proud to accept any meager crusts of comfort he might toss her now. Besides, how could she ever explain to him that she felt cheated because they had never wept in each other's arms over Caitlin? She couldn't even articulate why it mattered so much to her. Maybe she was being foolish. Or maybe she was crazy—still crazy with grief after all this time.

Doug stood up unceremoniously and jerked open the screen door. "I'm going in, Barb. Time to hit the sack. You coming?"

"Not now," she murmured distractedly. She felt

hurt, and he couldn't even see it. And she couldn't make him understand. Was she trying to punish him for not knowing instinctively what she really needed? "You go on in, Doug. I'll be along in a while."

His tone hardened. "Sure, Barbara. Why not?"

It was the same old story, each of them desperately needing something, but not what the other had to offer. As he stormed inside she heard him mutter to himself, "Why in blazes did I think tonight would be any different from any other night?"

She steeled herself, but jumped anyway when the screen door clattered shut behind him, leaving her sitting alone and cold in the wind-whispering darkness.

Chapter Twelve

After a jam-packed weekend of swimming, hiking and picnicking, on Sunday night Doug gathered his things, kissed Barbara and Janee goodbye and headed out to his car. Barbara walked with him, hating to see him go. It seemed they were just learning to relax and have fun as a family—and now he was leaving again.

When he suggested she and Janee ride back with him to pick up her car, she unthinkingly told him it wasn't necessary because Trent was glad to take her wherever she needed to go.

Doug merely frowned and mumbled something under his breath about his wife depending on an old beau and how it had better not become a habit. She kissed him and assured him he had nothing to worry about because she had eyes for only one man. He smiled back, but there was a sadness, a detachment, in his expression, as if he didn't quite believe her.

Or maybe he was remembering their clash on the porch on Friday night and the undercurrent of disappointment that had lingered, shadowing their time together.

On Monday afternoon Barbara discovered that the back door lock wouldn't work. She phoned Trent and asked if he could come over and fix it. He had always been a handyman at heart and could repair anything. "Be there in a jiffy," he told her, and five minutes later he was standing at her door with his toolbox.

While he worked on the lock, Barbara brewed him some coffee, and Janee regaled him with tales of her latest adventures. "When Uncle Doug was here, we saw a coyote in the woods," she enthused. "He was so cute, I wanted to pet him. But he ran away."

"Really?" said Trent. "Well, I'll tell you, gal, it's a good thing you didn't pet that little critter. They've got mighty sharp teeth."

"That's what Uncle Doug told me. But we did lots of other stuff. We went swimming at the lake. And Uncle Doug took us in a sailboat. It rocked back and forth, like this—" she demonstrated with her arms "—and my nose got sunburned."

"Sounds like you had quite a weekend for yourself, darlin'." Trent's smile flashed from Janee to

Barbara. "Lake Arrowhead's a mighty nice place to have fun, isn't it?"

"Oh, it was *so* much fun, Uncle Trent!"

He grinned. "So it's Uncle Trent now, is it?"

Barbara handed him his coffee. "To Janee, everyone's an aunt or uncle. I hope you don't mind."

"You kidding? I'm honored."

"And we had a picnic on the beach," Janee rushed on excitedly. "What was it called, Aunt Barbara?"

"Blue Jay Bay."

"Oh, yeah. We had hamburgers and potato chips and chocolate brownies. They were so good. And we went to the children's museum, and—"

"Janee, you'd better stop and catch your breath," Barbara urged. She poured herself a cup of coffee and sat down at the oak table near where Trent was working. "I've never heard her be such a little chatterbox."

"It's a sign of a happy child," said Trent with a note of wistfulness. "It shows you and Doug are doing something right. You're raising a wonderful little girl. I just wish Sheila and I could have had children."

Barbara stirred a spoonful of sugar into her coffee. "Doug and I never thought we'd have another chance...after Caitlin."

Trent smiled. "And look what God has done for you, giving you Janee."

Barbara nodded. It had never occurred to her that

Janee could be the answer to her prayers. She had spent much time thinking of Janee as an unwanted obligation suddenly thrust upon her, but surely not as a blessing. Yet somehow in the past week the child had become just that—an incredible blessing.

"Uncle Trent, can you stay and help us build nesting boxes?"

"Nesting boxes?"

Janee nodded, her little chin jutting out. "Yes! For all the baby chickadees and bluebirds and nuthatches that have no home."

Trent stood up and brushed off the knees of his jeans. "That sounds like quite a project to me. Sure, I'd be glad to help."

"I'm not quite sure how to go about it," said Barbara, "but I remember we used to make them when we were kids."

"Sure, darlin'. You and I made nesting boxes for the birds the summer you were twelve and I was fourteen."

"Yes, I remember. We were so idealistic, weren't we? That year we thought we could save every animal of the forest."

"We did a lot of good that summer. Helped a lot of birds and animals. And had a whole lot of fun doing it."

Barbara felt her cheeks grow pink. "I remember. Strange, isn't it? Suddenly it's all coming back as if it were yesterday."

"We had a lot of good times together, Barb. Sometimes I wish I could go back."

For the life of her, Barbara couldn't think of an appropriate response. Was Trent saying he wished he'd married her instead of Sheila? Or was he speaking out of a grieving heart that still mourned the wife he'd lost?

Janee saved the day by interrupting. "When are we going to make nesting boxes? I want to make them now!"

"And so we shall, kiddo," said Trent, taking Janee's hands and swinging her arms wide. "I'll go home and get some supplies and be right back. Think you can wait that long?"

"I don't know," Janee said seriously. "My hands and feet don't want to wait very long."

"Well, you do some jumping jacks until I get back. That'll keep your hands and feet so busy, they won't know they're waiting."

"Okay, Uncle Trent. I'll jump real high."

"And I'll be back soon," he promised.

Three hours later they were sitting on the kitchen floor putting the finishing touches on the nesting boxes, when Barbara heard the front doorbell. Looking in dismay at the door, she touched her mussed hair and looked down at her rumpled shirt. "Goodness, I'm not ready for company."

"I'll get it for you," said Trent, standing up and tucking in a loose shirttail.

Barbara continued working, absently listening as

Trent explained to the caller that the lady of the house was unavailable. She straightened up and listened when she heard a familiar voice say, "Isn't this the Logan cabin? Doug and Barbara Logan?" The voice was that of Benny Cotter, her brother-in-law!

Barbara scrambled to her feet and rushed to the door, intercepting Trent before he sent Pam and Benny on their way. Benny stood closest to the door, wearing his typical flashy suit and flashier tie. Pam stood a step behind, wearing an expensive mint-green suit, her thick ebony hair professionally styled. She looked as immaculate as ever.

"Pam! Benny!" Barbara exclaimed. "For goodness' sake! Come in! I never expected to see the two of you up here."

"Thought we had the wrong house for a minute," said Benny, eyeing Trent skeptically.

Trent smiled sheepishly and eased himself away from the door, giving Barbara a look that said, *Whoops, my mistake!*

"Please, come in and sit down," Barbara urged. Benny stepped inside and Pam followed, moving gingerly in her three-inch heels. "Pam and Benny, I'd like you to meet Trent Townsend. He lives next door."

As they shook hands, Pam said, "The name sounds familiar. Have we met before, Mr. Townsend?"

"Could be. If you've been up to the cabin before.

My family has owned the place next door since I was a kid.''

Pam touched a long, polished nail to her shiny red lips. ''That's it! You're Barbara's friend. The young man she was dating when she met my brother.''

''One and the same,'' he replied dryly.

''What a coincidence. Imagine her running into you again now that she and Doug are separated.''

''We're not separated, Pam,'' Barbara corrected. ''We're living apart temporarily because of the earthquake.''

''Oh, that's what I meant, Barb. Not *separated!* You know I didn't mean to suggest you were having trouble in your marriage.''

Janee appeared from the kitchen and gazed shyly at Pam and Benny. Pam spotted her and scooped the child up in her arms. ''Look, Benny. Here's our little sweetheart, looking pretty as a fairy princess. How are you, Janee?''

Janee lowered her gaze. ''Me and Aunt Barbara and Uncle Trent are making nesting boxes for the little birdies. Do you wanna come see?''

''Uncle Trent?'' echoed Benny with a note of skepticism.

''She calls everyone that,'' said Barbara lamely. She could read the terrible misconceptions already forming in Benny's mind, and they made her cringe. Benny always had a way of putting the worst spin on things.

"We'll come see them after a while, honey," said Pam, shifting Janee in her arms. It was obvious she didn't know how to carry a child. "Right now we've come to talk to your Aunt Barbara," she said, her tone artificially sweet.

Trent went over and took Janee from Pam. "We'll go take the nesting boxes outside and find a place to put them, right, gal?"

Janee clapped her hands as they headed for the kitchen.

Barbara removed a newspaper and one of Janee's dolls from the sofa. "Sit down and relax. Can I get you something? A soft drink? Coffee? I could fix you a sandwich or something."

"No, nothing for us," replied Pam. "We ate on the way up the mountain." When Janee and Trent were out of sight, Pam leaned forward and said confidentially, "We've come in answer to your call, Barb."

Barbara stared at them in confusion. "My call?"

"Yes. You called us a couple of weeks ago about taking Janee off your hands. We didn't think we'd be able to do it, but I was laid off from my accounting job last week, so Benny and I had this talk, you know? And we decided that I'll stay home and take care of his bookkeeping. You know, for his used car dealership. I mean, I was helping him some before, but now I'll be able to do it full-time. At home. So don't you see? I'll have lots of time to take care of a child. Of Janee. In fact, Benny and I think it might be kind of fun. Something we haven't done before. A whole new adventure. Aren't you pleased?''

Barbara was still two steps behind. ''You—You came all the way from Oregon to pick up Janee?''

''Well, not just to pick up Janee,'' Pam conceded. ''Actually, Benny's here on a business trip.''

''I'm here to scout out the used car market,'' Benny interjected. ''You know what they say about L.A.—the used car capital of the world.''

''And so I decided to join him,'' said Pam, her voice sounding like a kitten's purr. ''Like I said, we came so we could get Janee. Only, of course, you weren't home—and, oh, Barbara, it's a terrible shame about your house. Doug called us when it happened, but we never dreamed...I mean, once we saw it, you know, we were just shocked. It's a crying shame!''

''A stroke of luck that you have this cabin,'' said Benny. ''Of course, it's a little rough around the edges, but—''

''We've actually enjoyed it,'' said Barbara. ''Janee and me both.''

''But it must be hard being away from Doug for days at a time.'' A sly smile crept across Pam's lips. ''Of course, I see you didn't waste any time renewing old acquaintanceships, if you know what I mean.''

''I know exactly what you mean,'' Barbara said coolly. ''And believe me, Pam, it was pure coincidence that Trent and I ran into each other. He's been a kind and helpful neighbor—and that's all.''

Pam raised a conciliatory hand. ''Oh, Barbara, I believe you. Really, I was just speaking in jest. Trying for a little levity. But I'm not good at that like Benny. You must know I would never suggest that there was any impropriety going on between you and your old flame.'' She stifled a smile. ''No matter how gorgeous he is.''

Benny guffawed and reached over and squeezed Pam's knee. ''You keep your eyes on your number one man, you hear?''

Barbara forced the indignation out of her voice. ''Pam, Benny, you came here to talk about Janee. So let me have my say.''

''Certainly, Barbara. The floor is yours,'' said Benny.

Barbara inhaled deeply. Why did she suddenly feel that she was facing a judge and jury? ''First of all, let me thank you both for responding to my phone call. At the time I was feeling rather overwhelmed with my life, and I thought—I just thought maybe Janee would be better off with someone else…with the two of you.''

''And we've come to see that you're absolutely right,'' said Pam, her smile brilliant as a neon sign.

''But that's just it,'' Barbara protested. ''I wasn't right. I was wrong. Since we came to the cabin, Janee has settled in very well. We're getting along wonderfully. We're very happy together.''

Pam crossed her long, tapered legs with a practiced grace. "But, Barbara, dear, what can you offer a child in a moldering old cabin like this, stuck in the backwoods on top of some mountain? Janee belongs in the city where she can have the best school, the finest clothes, the right friends."

"She'll have all of that as soon as we get settled back into our home. Meanwhile, we're having a pleasant little vacation together in this rustic cabin—which isn't moldering in the least."

Pam tapped her long fingernails on the tufted arm of the sofa. "Well, Barbara, I just wish you had phoned us and told us you'd changed your mind. You would have saved me a trip."

"I didn't hear from you, Pam, so I just assumed you weren't interested."

"I'll tell you what," said Benny. "We bought a plane ticket for the kid, so we might as well take her back with us for a week. Give you a little break."

Barbara stiffened. "You want to take Janee home with you? Now?"

"Just for a week," said Pam smoothly. "After all, we haven't had a chance to get to know our little niece, have we? Surely you're not going to begrudge us a week with her." Pam's tone took on a cutting edge. "I mean, a couple of weeks ago you were ready to pawn her off on us for good."

Barbara's temper flared, but she clenched her

teeth and said evenly, "I wasn't trying to pawn her off on you. I was just—"

"Yeah, we get the picture," said Benny. "So how about it? We take the kid now, and you get her back in a week. Fair enough?"

Barbara's mind raced. There was a certain inevitable logic in their reasoning. And surely they had as much right to spend time with Janee as she did. But at the back of Barbara's mind a warning light flashed. "I really hate to uproot the child again, Pam," she said, trying not to let her rising emotion color her voice. "You know how it is. She's just gotten comfortable here at the cabin."

"Oh, for Pete's sake, Barbara, children are adaptable. They're resilient. I may not have kids, but everyone knows that."

Suddenly Janee peeked her head in the doorway and asked eagerly, "When are you going to come outside and see my nesting boxes?"

Benny stood up. "In just a minute, sweetheart."

"Me and Uncle Trent found the neatest little cave. We put a nesting box in it. Wanna come see?"

"Sure, kiddo," said Benny. "Hey, where's your, uh, your Uncle Trent?"

"He went home."

"Smart man," said Pam. "He knows when it's time to retreat."

"Hey, listen, Janee," said Benny. "The nesting boxes can wait, okay? Your Aunt Pam and I have a surprise for you. Come here, honey, and see your Uncle Benny."

Janee shuffled over to him, looking shy but curious. Benny picked her up in his arms and bounced her up and down. "Hey, pretty girl, how would you like to come visit your Aunt Pam and Uncle Benny in Oregon for a few days?"

Janee cast a questioning glance at Barbara. Before Barbara could respond, Pam was on her feet. In those deadly three-inch heels, she sashayed over to Benny and clasped Janee's round cheeks in her palms. "You'll have lots of fun, honey," she purred as she smoothed Janee's flyaway hair. "We'll ride on a big airplane, and when we get home we'll go to the toy store and you can buy any toy you want."

Janee's eyes grew wide as saucers. "Can I buy a baby doll that drinks and wets?"

Benny guffawed. "Sweetheart, you can buy a doll that dances, juggles plates, and sings 'God Bless America,' if you like."

Janee shook her head solemnly. "No, just one that drinks and wets."

"Janee's not going anywhere," said Barbara under her breath. Her eyes were shooting darts at Benny, but he chose not to notice.

"Let's see what Janee wants to do," said Benny with the flashy, inflated tone of a salesman closing a deal. "What about it, Janee? You want to come home with Pam and me?"

Janee's cheeks glowed with anticipation. "Will we go to the toy store and buy my dolly?"

"That's a promise, kiddo. And your Uncle Benny never goes back on a promise."

Janee looked over at Barbara and a shadow crossed her face. "Can Aunt Barbara come, too?"

"Not this time, baby," said Pam. "But we'll bring you right back to your Aunt Barbara whenever you want to come. Okay?"

Janee twisted her mouth as if deep in thought. Finally she grinned and said, "Okay."

"Great! Pam, you go help Janee pack a few of her clothes." Benny set Janee down and patted her head. "Now, you scoot along, gal." He looked at Pam. "She won't need much, hon. We'll buy her some new stuff."

Barbara stepped forward and seized Janee's hand. "Wait just a minute. I don't think Janee's going anywhere. She's better off staying right here."

"Really?" challenged Benny, fingering his too-wide red tie. "Why don't you ask Janee what she wants to do?"

Barbara stood immobilized for a moment. Benny had her in a corner. No matter what she said now in her own defense, she was going to come off looking like the bad guy. "You two are making this very difficult..."

Janee clasped Barbara's arms and pleaded, "Please, Aunt Barbara, please, let me go! Please, please, please!"

Barbara gathered Janee up in her arms. Janee bounced and rocked and begged, "Please, Aunt Barbara, pretty please with sugar on it!"

Tears welled in Barbara's eyes. She embraced Janee tightly and kissed the top of her golden hair. "You really want to go, sweet girl?"

Janee gave her an exaggerated nod. "Yes, Aunt Barbara. I'm going to get a dolly that drinks and wets."

Reluctantly Barbara set Janee down. "Okay, baby, go to your room and get your favorite clothes and put them in your backpack." As Janee scampered off, Barbara turned a withering gaze on Pam and Benny. "I don't appreciate the two of you coming in here unannounced and persuading Janee to go home with you. She's just a five-year-old, and you manipulated her. That's inexcusable."

"Oh, Barbara, don't be so stuffy," said Pam, examining one long crimson nail. "For someone who wanted to unload the kid a couple of weeks ago, you're sure acting the concerned mommy now. Besides, it's just a week. The kid will have a great time. She'll be back here before you know it."

"One week," said Barbara coldly. She was trembling, but she didn't want them to notice. "I want that child back in this cabin one week from today."

"Sure," said Pam breezily. "I'll bring her myself. And don't worry. We'll treat her like a little princess."

Benny motioned to Pam. "Go help the kid pack,

okay? I want to get back down the mountain before nightfall."

Before Barbara could quite comprehend what was happening, Janee was traipsing out the door with Pam and Benny. Barbara stood on the porch and watched, stunned and speechless, as they buckled Janee into the back seat and drove off down the road in their fancy rental car.

When their automobile was out of sight, the reality of what had just happened struck Barbara like a sudden punch in the stomach. She nearly doubled over as she stumbled back inside the cabin. "Oh, Janee," her voice echoed eerily in the empty cabin. "Janee, baby, how could I let them take you?"

She hurried to her cell phone and called Doug at the hospital. "He doesn't answer his page," said the operator.

"Keep trying." Barbara was shaking so hard now that her teeth nearly chattered.

After nearly ten minutes, Doug came on the line. "What's up, Barb?"

"They've come and taken Janee," she blurted.

Doug's voice rang with alarm. "Who took her? What are you talking about, Barb?"

"Pam and Benny." She was weeping now. "They came here, Doug. Out of the blue. They showed up at the cabin and said they had decided to take Janee. Just like that. They just drove off with her. They're taking her home to Oregon."

"Barb, I don't understand. They've never wanted

kids. They certainly didn't want Janee. Why on earth would they come and take her now?"

"I don't know," Barbara said between sobs. "Maybe because I—I called and asked them to take her."

"You asked them to take her? What kind of fool thing—!"

"I know, Doug. I was wrong. Terribly wrong. But that was weeks ago, before the earthquake. Before we came here. Before I realized how much I want Janee to stay with us."

"Then why didn't you just tell them no?"

"I tried, but they promised Janee the world, and she wanted to go. What could I say?"

"Okay, calm down, Barb. You know Pam and Benny. A child would cramp their style, they know that. I'm sure they don't plan to keep her for long."

"They said it's just for a week," Barbara said shakily. "But I don't believe them, Doug. I have a bad feeling about this. I think they intend to keep Janee for good. Oh, Doug, I don't think they'll ever let us have her back!"

Chapter Thirteen

In the days that followed, Barbara felt as if she were caught in a time warp and moving in slow motion. Worse, she was slogging through the depths of despair. Each day was longer than the one before. The tedium was nearly unbearable.

She missed Janee. Heavens, how she missed that child. The cabin that had rung with the little girl's laughter and been bright with her smile was suddenly a desolate place. How could it be, Barbara wondered, that she found herself in the untenable predicament of grieving for two children? Her beloved Caitlin was gone and could never come back, of course. But Janee—precious Janee—the child she had almost let slip through her fingers. Janee belonged here with Barbara. Janee had to come home again. Had to!

As the week dragged on, Barbara considered leaving the cabin and returning to Los Angeles. She and Doug could rent an apartment until their house was ready, or even stay in a motel. But she couldn't quite bear the thought of leaving this cabin where she and Janee had learned to care for each other. Leaving would break that special connection she felt with the child. Here in this homey cabin they had played and read and sung and prayed together. Here, for the first time, Barbara had discovered she could actually love another child.

But what irony. Now that she wanted Janee, Pam and Benny had decided they wanted her, too. Was God punishing her for her anger and bitterness and resentment over Caitlin's death?

For four long years Barbara had nursed those dark, insidious emotions. Her anger had revealed itself in ways subtle—and not so subtle. Grief had erected a wall between her and Doug, between her and God. After losing Caitlin, she had locked her heart against them both, partly in self-defense, partly as a means of striking back at them.

And yet she was never quite sure why she felt the need to retaliate. Did she believe Doug was responsible for Caitlin's death? Was God responsible? She wasn't sure. She knew only that someone was to blame. The worst moment of her life couldn't have been a random, meaningless incident.

By Friday Barbara was fit to be tied. She had phoned Pam and Benny every day and left messages on their machine, but they never returned her calls.

What was going on? She had visions of them skipping the country, disappearing forever with Janee to some remote island, some foreign continent. What if she never saw Janee again?

How was it possible that she had finally allowed a chink in her stony heart that would allow it to be shattered again by a child she had never meant to care for?

In desperation Barbara finally took out her Bible and sat down to read. So often when she was troubled she resisted reading the Scriptures; she told herself it wouldn't help. She wasn't in the mood; the verses wouldn't be relevant to her situation. But inevitably when she started reading a passage, she would feel the tug of God's Spirit, and she would realize this was what she should have been doing all along.

It was that way now, too. As she thumbed through the Book of Romans, she felt a hunger to make amends with God. She had held her heart back from Him for so long, but He was still there, waiting, ready to shower her with His love. She knew this instinctively, knew it with every fiber of her being, and yet she resisted God, turned from His love.

What was wrong with her that she couldn't give in and let God be God in her life? Why couldn't she simply open her hands and let Him have His way in her heart? Was it too important to nurse her grief, to clutch her anger to her breast?

As she scanned the eighth chapter of Romans,

several verses caught her attention. She read them aloud, hungrily, the very words a balm to her wounded heart. "'For I reckon that the sufferings of this present time are not worthy to be compared with the glory which shall be revealed in us.... Likewise the Spirit also helpeth our infirmities.... And we know that all things work together for good to them that love God, to them who are the called according to His purpose.'"

Barbara closed the Bible and moved her fingertips over its sturdy binding. *Dear God, if only I had the kind of faith to believe that everything in my life is working together for good. If only I could trust You again—but I can't. I'm so afraid. What if You demand more of me than I can give? I can't bear any more losses. I'm sorry, God, I just can't!*

Barbara set the Bible back in the bookcase as tears brimmed in her eyes. "Oh, Lord," she whispered, "I want to love You. I want to trust You. I want to love Doug again the way I used to. I don't want my heart to be like stone. Please, help me! I can't do it by myself!" She sank down on the floor beside the sofa, cradled her head in her arms and wept. As her tears flowed, she had the extraordinary sensation that she wasn't alone, that someone—God Himself—was holding her in His arms, offering His solace.

She cried until her tears were spent, then rested her head on the sofa cushion and savored God's comforting presence. "You are here for me, after all,'' she murmured. ''You understand how weak I am. You know I can't go it alone.''

When she had finished praying, Barbara stood up and dried her eyes, then went to the bathroom and touched up her face. Her eyes were red-rimmed, but she felt amazingly refreshed. God had given her a new lease on life. He would see her through, she knew now, whatever happened.

And He would bring Janee safely back to her, for hadn't He brought Janee into her life in the first place? Surely God wouldn't tantalize her with a child, then tear that child from her arms. He wouldn't do that to her again. He knew how much she had suffered over Caitlin. If there truly was a time for every season under heaven, surely now it was her time to be happy.

Barbara was running a brush through her hair when she heard the doorbell ring. Maybe it was Pam and Benny bringing Janee back a few days early. Wouldn't that be a perfect answer to her prayers? She tossed the brush aside and hurried to the front door. Her heart sank when she spotted Trent Townsend through the screen. ''Hi,'' she said, trying to hide her disappointment. ''Come on in.''

''Thanks. Don't mind if I do.'' He opened the screen door and sauntered inside. He was wearing a polo shirt and slacks, and looked like he was ready for a game of tennis. ''What's up, Barb?'' he asked. ''You look like you were expecting someone, and I'm afraid it wasn't me.''

"I'm sorry. I thought it might be Pam and Benny bringing Janee back. I should have known better. It hasn't been a week yet." She gestured toward the sofa. "Sit down. Can I get you some iced tea?"

"No, thanks. I'm fine." He sat down and stretched out his long legs. "You miss her, don't you?"

"More than I dreamed possible. I never thought I'd feel this way again about a child. I guess I would never let myself. I was too afraid of being hurt again."

Trent nodded, his gray-green eyes shadowed. "I know what you mean. I wish I could care for someone again the way I cared about Sheila. But right now I can't even imagine it."

Barbara sat down beside Trent and touched his arm. "Don't lock your heart to the possibilities. That's what I did, Trent. After Caitlin died, I built a wall around myself. I wouldn't let anyone in. Not Doug, not God, not even another child who needed love. But somehow, when I came to this cabin with Janee, God broke through and showed me I could open my heart to love again. He'll show you, too, if you let Him."

"I'm not a praying man, Barb. I wouldn't even know what to say."

"That's the beauty of it, Trent. If you just open your heart to His love, He gives you the words. Try it sometime."

He grinned. "Sure, why not? If it works for you, who knows?"

"It's not just glib advice, Trent. I've spent this afternoon wrestling with God over my own hurt and anger. And He made me realize He really is there for me. The Bible says, 'If God is for us, who can be against us?'"

"A good motto to live by," Trent agreed.

"Wait, there's another one. I'm a little rusty at this, but it went something like this. 'If God gave His own Son for us, won't He also freely give us everything we need?'"

"That does have a certain poetic ring."

"All my life I've believed that God gave His Son to die for me, Trent, but I rarely think about all the other things He gives us. Maybe I've just never let the simple truth of His love penetrate my heart. I've gotten so used to thinking of God as someone who snatches good things away from us. Like Caitlin. Like Sheila. But that's not the God the Bible speaks of. It says our God is a God who freely gives us all things."

Trent chuckled. "Keep it up, Barb, and I'll get you your own pulpit."

She stifled a smile. "I was preaching, wasn't I? And you know I'm not usually one to wear my faith on my sleeve."

"That's okay. I can use all the good words I can get."

Barbara shook her head, marveling. "Usually my

attitude is, Live and let live. But today was a real breakthrough for me. And I know you're struggling with the same deep grief."

Trent raked his fingers through his hair. "I know there's an answer out there for me, too, but it's going to take me a while to find it." He squeezed her shoulder. "You and Janee have been a real help. Just spending time with the two of you these past couple of weeks has helped me see there's still a life out there for me—somewhere...with someone."

"You'll find it," Barbara assured him. "Or should I say, you'll find *her,* whoever and wherever she is."

"Maybe." Trent stood up and Barbara followed. "Listen, I almost forgot the reason I came over," he said with a crinkly-eyed smile. "I was wondering if you wanted to run out and grab a bite to eat with me. Nothing fancy. A pizza maybe, or a couple of burgers."

"I'm sorry, I can't, Trent. Doug will be driving up tonight. I was thinking of fixing him something special."

"Sure, I understand. You're a great gal, Barb. I never should have let you get away." He drew her gently into his arms. She resisted for a moment, then relented. After all, it was just a comforting embrace between friends. "Thanks for being here for me, Barb. You've been a godsend."

"Thanks, Trent."

He was still holding her when she heard the doorbell ring. Was it Janee this time? She looked over and saw Doug through the screen door. His expression was sullen and his eyes bored through the screen at the two of them.

Trent released her, and she stepped back awkwardly. "Doug," she exclaimed, "I didn't expect you this soon."

He came inside, letting the screen door slam shut behind him. "That's obvious. Maybe I should give you two a little more time. Or maybe I've given you too much time already." He said it as if he were making a joke, but there was a bite in his tone.

"Hey, ol' man, I'm on my way out." Trent gave Doug a good-natured tap on the shoulder. "Take good care of our girl here. She's one in a million."

"You're not telling me anything I don't already know." Doug walked Trent to the door and pushed it open. "You have a good night now, Trent."

"I intend to." Trent looked back and waved, then walked off into the night whistling to himself.

Doug locked the screen door. "That man irritates the life out of me."

Barbara went to her husband and kissed him lightly on the lips. "You almost sound jealous, darling."

He pulled her into his arms. "Not jealous. Just...I don't know."

"Trent is part of my past. You know that. He's just a friend. And after losing Sheila, *he* needs a friend."

"Does it have to be you?"

"I didn't plan it that way. We just somehow ended up neighbors again after all these years."

Doug nuzzled the top of her head. "Well, just make sure he doesn't get too neighborly."

She laughed in spite of herself. "You are jealous, aren't you? I can't believe it—my husband jealous of an old boyfriend."

"Not jealous!"

She looked at him. "Yes, you are. It's as obvious as the scowl on your face." With her fingertips she traced the line of his lips. He had a full, sensuous mouth she had always loved to kiss. And yet it had been months—no, years—since they had kissed with the passionate abandon of teenagers. Was that Doug's fault? Or hers? "Darling," she said, tenderly. "If I'd wanted Trent, I would have married him instead of you. It's you I wanted. Only you."

He held her more tightly. He was obviously pleased with her declaration of love, but he would never admit it. "You're in a good mood, Barbie. Did something happen?"

"Only in my heart," she murmured. She wanted to spill out every detail of her spiritual journey today—her prayers, the passages of Scripture that had touched her heart, the amazing sensation that God was holding her in His arms and comforting her. But she couldn't find the words. There was no way to explain how God had finally broken through the stony wall of her heart and filled her with His love and peace. At last she could begin to trust Him with her life, her hopes and dreams. But the experience was too fresh, too fragile to confine with mere words.

"Barbie, we've got to talk." There was a disturbing edge to Doug's voice. Something was wrong.

She searched his eyes. "What is it? What happened? Is it the house? Not another earthquake. I haven't had the television on, but surely I would have felt something here."

"Not an earthquake. Not the house."

"Then what?"

"Sit down, hon." He led her over to the sofa, and they sat down stiffly, facing each other. His hand moved to her shoulder. He massaged her neck, kneading the muscles with a nervous, repetitive gesture, as if he were concentrating hard on something else, far removed. "It's Janee."

"Janee?" Barbara's heart stopped. "Is she hurt?"

"No, she's fine. I didn't mean to alarm you."

Barbara smiled with relief. "Doug, you scoundrel, you scared me. Now tell me. What about Janee?"

Doug's lips tightened. There was a weariness around his eyes she hadn't noticed before. He inhaled sharply and said, "Pam and Benny won't be bringing Janee home."

"Won't bring her home? What are you talking about? They've got to bring her home!"

"I'm afraid they don't see it that way, Barb. I don't know how to say this—"

"Just tell me, Doug!"

"Pam and Benny have petitioned the court. They want to adopt Janee."

Barbara scoffed, her throat letting out a little explosion of laughter. "Adopt Janee? Pam and Benny? You must be kidding!"

Deep furrows marred Doug's forehead and his dusky blue eyes glinted with rancor. "I wish I were, Barb. I'm sorry. It's not a joke. Pam and Benny are dead serious."

"How do you know? Did they tell you so?"

"I was served with papers today. From their lawyer. There'll be a court hearing, Barb. A judge in San Francisco will decide who keeps Janee."

"But how can that be?" Barbara shook her head in bewilderment. "We have Janee. The will said so. We're her guardians."

"Her legal guardians, yes, but we've made no petition for adoption. Now Pam and Benny have."

"But why? Why would they want her now?" Barbara cried.

"I don't know. Maybe she somehow awakened their maternal and paternal instincts."

"You don't believe that any more than I do."

"If it didn't sound a bit malicious, I'd say Benny's got his eyes on Janee's trust fund. Whoever adopts her would have control over it until she's twenty-one."

"Why would Pam and Benny want Janee's money? They're wealthy."

Doug nodded. "The way they live, you'd think they're rolling in dough. But maybe the used car business isn't what it used to be. Maybe they're overextended. Who knows? I just feel there has to be a financial motive behind their sudden interest in Janee."

"How can we find out?"

"I don't know. If you want to fight this—"

"Of course, I want to fight it. I want Janee. Don't you?"

"Yes, I've wanted her from the beginning, but I wasn't sure how you felt."

"I want her, Doug." Barbara's voice broke with emotion. "I love her. I never knew I could love a child again."

"Then we'll have to get ourselves a lawyer."

"We have a lawyer."

"A corporate attorney. But we need someone who can win this case for us."

"Where do we begin?"

"We'll do what Pam and Benny did. File a petition to adopt Janee, to make her our own little girl."

"What if they win, Doug?"

"We won't let them, Barbie. Janee's ours."

Barbara closed her eyes and pressed her fingertips against her throbbing temples. "Oh, Doug, it's happening all over again, isn't it? We're losing the child we love." A sob tore from her throat. "Just when I thought I could trust God again!"

Doug pulled her to him and wrapped her in his warm, strong arms. "There, there, Barbie. It'll be okay. We've got to believe it'll all work out right."

"No, Doug. I can't bear it. I can't live through it again. I'd rather be dead than face that pain again."

His arms tightened around her. "We'll get through it, Barbie," he whispered, his voice raw with emotion. "I promise. God help us, we'll have our Janee back if it's the last thing we do."

Chapter Fourteen

Throughout the weekend Barbara could think of only one thing: Pam and Benny were going to take Janee away from her. That dreadful possibility darkened her time with Doug. How could either of them put on a happy face with such a threat looming? How could Doug's own flesh and blood pull such a vile trick? Worse, how could God allow this to happen when Barbara had just made her peace with Him after all these years?

Such bitter irony belonged in some Greek tragedy. Imagine, just when she had decided to trust God completely, He had pulled the rug out from under her again.

On Monday morning, after a quiet, solemn weekend at the cabin, Doug packed his small valise and prepared once again to drive back down the mountain. As Barbara walked with him to his car, he urged her to come with him. "This place is so lonely and isolated, Barb. Why don't you just throw a few things into a bag, lock the door and ride back with me? Maybe you'd feel better in town with all its hustle and bustle. It would keep your mind off things."

She declined. "It would mean lonely days in some dreary motel room while you work long hours at the hospital. No, I'd rather remain here in the cabin. It's filled with happy memories of my days here with Janee."

"Are you sure you're not just torturing yourself?"

"Maybe, maybe not. I just know I can't leave."

"Okay. Have it your way." Doug embraced her, gave her a brief kiss on the lips and climbed into the driver's seat. "I'll make a few calls today and get the ball rolling to get Janee back in our custody until the court hearing." He shut the door and rolled down the window. "The way I see it, until a judge declares otherwise, we're her legal guardians."

Barbara leaned into the open window. "Please, Doug, do whatever's necessary. Get her back as soon as you can."

As he drove away, she felt a twinge of regret. Maybe she *should* have gone with him. What was she going to do in the empty cabin until he returned? She'd go stir-crazy, for sure. She stood with arms crossed as a chill breeze rippled through her cotton shirt. Doug's car was out of sight now, but she didn't move. She felt frail and painfully vulnerable, as if the buffeting winds might topple her, send her over the edge.

Barbara spent the afternoon looking at Janee's scrawled crayon drawings and her quaint pinecone people with the felt hats and coats. Awash with nostalgia, she took magnets and placed several of the drawings on the refrigerator door, remembering how Nancy's refrigerator had dazzled with Janee's colorful renderings. Barbara mentally replayed the hours she and Janee had spent going for walks in the woods and feeding the squirrels and building nesting boxes. She retraced every memory of Janee she could summon, until a knot of anguish tightened in her chest, so painful she had to stop and catch her breath.

At last she ambled over to the window and looked out at the red sunset blazing through the silhouetted pines. Aloud she said, "What do You want of me, God? Is this a game You're playing? Testing me to see what it takes to break me? I'll tell You. It won't take much. I'm at my wits' end, and I don't know how long I can hang on."

She brushed away an uninvited tear. "Are You really there, God?" she whispered. "Do You love me? Then help me, because I can't help myself. I can't spend my days being all maudlin and weepy. I've lost too much time mourning for Caitlin. I can't do it for Janee, too. Lord, help me to get through this. Please, help me!"

She waited, silent, hardly breathing, listening for the sound of God's voice in her heart. She heard only the wind in the eaves and the caw of a bird in flight. Just as she was about to despair, the thought came to her, *No matter what I take from you, you will always have Me, and I am sufficient.*

The words rang in her heart, as stunning and remarkable as if she had heard them aloud. *Learn in your heart of hearts that I am enough. I can meet your needs no matter what else happens to you. No matter what you lose, you have everything in Me.*

The idea was revolutionary, that she could lose everything she cherished and God would still meet her needs. He would be her all in all.

"I want to believe it, Lord. Please, help me. And help me to live it, Father."

Every day for the rest of the week Barbara prayed and meditated on God's Word. She found herself feeling refreshed and able to cope with the uncertainties surrounding Janee. It was such a simple thing, spending time alone with God, and yet it made all the difference in her outlook. How could she have been a Christian all these years and yet have missed this vital truth?

When Doug arrived on Friday night she was eager to tell him of her spiritual odyssey. But before she could find the words, he announced with a broad smile, "Pam and Benny are flying down tomorrow. They're bringing Janee home."

"Oh, Doug, thank God!" She flew into his arms,

and he swung her around. Her mind reeled with euphoria. But after a few heady moments, the questions tumbled in. "Does this mean they've dropped the petition to adopt Janee? Can we keep her, Doug?"

A reluctant frown erased the earlier laugh lines. "I'm sorry, Barb. It's just temporary. Until our court date. I've lined up a good attorney—Randolph Tate. He reminded Benny's lawyer that we're Janee's legal guardians and they can't keep her without our permission."

"But we still have to go to San Francisco and fight it out in court?"

"Looks that way. San Francisco was Janee's home, and that's where the will was probated. The court there holds jurisdiction. So we'll have to fly up early next month."

"When?"

"Tuesday. The fifteenth."

"And if the judge says they can have Janee...?"

"We'll cross that bridge when we come to it. Meanwhile, we'll build the best case possible." Doug shrugged off his herringbone jacket and loosened his tie. "I did some checking, Barb. Nothing official. Just some private inquiries."

She looked quizzically at him. "You checked on Pam and Benny?"

"More specifically, Cotter Motors. I have a few banker friends in high places. I learned via the grapevine that Benny's business is in financial trouble, Barb. Some bad debts. I don't know what all. Anyway, Benny's been trying to get a loan, but he was turned down. Word has it he was inquiring whether he could borrow against Janee's trust fund."

Barbara put her hand to her throat. "You're saying all Janee is to him is a meal ticket?"

"We have no proof, but that's my guess."

"We've got to tell the judge."

"It could get tricky, Barb. It could seem like we're just trying to smear Benny's name, and we could end up looking like the bad guy."

"Then, what can we do?"

"Just plead our case as honestly as we can." He drew her into the circle of his arms. "And trust God for the rest."

It was late Saturday afternoon before Benny's rented limousine pulled up beside the cabin. Barbara had been watching for them for hours, her impatience growing along with her anxieties. When she saw Janee jump out of the back seat, she dashed outside to meet the little girl on the porch and scooped her up in her arms.

"Aunt Barbara!" Janee squealed, wrapping her arms around Barbara's neck. "Zowie and I missed you so much!"

"Oh, honey, I missed you so much! And Zowie, too."

Doug came outside and greeted Janee with a hug,

then turned his gaze to his sister and her husband. "Hello, Pam," he said coolly. "Hello, Benny."

They all greeted one another with an icy reserve, then filed inside, Janee rushing ahead to reclaim her little pinecone family. Barbara offered refreshments—coffee and sandwiches—but Benny said no, they had to go. They had a return flight that evening. His voice held a note of embarrassment, unease. He kept tapping his fingers and looking around, as if seeking a way of escape.

After the shenanigans you've pulled, you deserve to squirm, Barbara thought ruefully, but she kept a polite smile in place, refusing to stoop to Benny's level. "You're sure you don't want some coffee?"

"Okay, maybe a cup," said Benny. He sat down on the sofa, stiffly, not allowing himself to settle back against the cushions.

Pam sat down beside him. "I'll have a cup, too. Black."

"I'll get the coffee," said Barbara. "Then the four of us need to talk this thing out. There has to be some way we can come to an understanding."

"No deal," said Benny. "Our attorney advised us not to discuss the case with you."

"For crying out loud, Benny," said Doug. "We're family." He sat down in the rocker across from Pam. "Surely you're not going along with this nonsense, sis."

Pam averted her gaze, her immaculately made-up face as inscrutable as a china doll's.

Barbara looked over at Janee, who was sitting by the fireplace playing with her pinecone family. "We'll have to talk later. Little pitchers have big ears."

After Barbara served the coffee, she took Janee by the hand and said, "It's time for bed, honey. Why don't you go wash up and get your pajamas on, and I'll come tuck you in."

Reluctantly Janee said her good-nights and trudged off to the bedroom with Zowie in tow.

When she had gone, Pam said in her honey-sweet voice, "Barbara, I hope you don't take it personally, our wanting to adopt Janee."

Barbara sat down in the overstuffed chair beside the sofa. "How am I supposed to take it, Pam? You know how much we want to keep Janee."

Pam bristled. "I know no such thing! In fact, you're the one who telephoned me several weeks ago and told me you couldn't stand living with that child. You didn't want her in your house for another day. You were beside yourself. You begged Benny and me to come take Janee off your hands. Well, that's what we're doing. You're getting exactly what you asked for."

Barbara's pulse raced. "I never meant—I was confused, Pam. I thought Janee hated me. I thought she'd be better off with you."

"And we think so, too, Barbara." Pam sipped her coffee, her pinky cocked delicately in the air. "We know you could never love another child after Caitlin. That's perfectly understandable. Janee was a painful reminder of the child you lost. No one would expect you to live with a youngster who brought you such grief." Pam's tone took on a smugly self-righteous air. "That's why we've decided to adopt Janee. We want her, even if you don't."

Barbara's indignation flared. "How dare you, Pam! I never said I—" She heard a rustling sound in the hallway and craned her neck around. "Janee, is that you?"

Janee's cherubic face peered around the corner. Her eyes were round and shiny as dinner plates, and her mouth formed a quivery pucker.

"I told you it's time for bed, honey," Barbara reminded her gently. "Now run along, sweetie. You need your sleep."

Without a word Janee disappeared down the hall.

After a lull the conversation returned to the impending court case. Benny cleared his throat and loosened his yellow, polka-dot tie. "Barbara, we could avoid this whole nasty battle if you and Doug would just relinquish custody of Janee and let us adopt her."

"We'll do no such thing," said Doug. "How you have the nerve to—"

"Please, Doug, be a good sport," urged Pam, her voice fawning, her crimson lips in a pout. "With Nancy gone, you're the only family I have. You're my big brother. We've got to stick together, right?

And you always said Benny and I should have kids. So now we will.''

Doug straightened his shoulders and thrust out his jaw, his eyes narrowing. ''You're ignoring one important fact, Pam. Nancy wanted Barbara and me to raise Janee.''

''But if you weren't able to take her, she wanted us to have her.''

''We are able and willing,'' said Doug. ''More than willing.''

''But that wasn't Barbara's story a few weeks ago,'' said Pam, her words knife-sharp but her voice still smooth as cream. ''I don't think it makes for a very stable home when your wife keeps going back and forth, changing her mind so drastically. Who's to say she won't change her mind again next week and decide she doesn't want Janee, after all. A child needs adults she can depend on, Doug.''

''She can depend on us, Pam, and you know it.''

Pam leisurely sipped her coffee. ''Well, I guess a judge will have to decide that, won't he?''

''You know you can't win, Pam.'' Barbara's voice broke on a sudden wave of emotion. ''In the hospital Nancy's dying request was that we take Janee. No judge would go against her last wishes.''

''Maybe not, but a lot has changed since Nancy died,'' Pam remarked.

''What are you talking about, Pam?'' challenged Doug.

Pam gazed steadily at him, her glossy lips unsmiling. "Well, for one thing, brother dear, you no longer have a home for Janee, thanks to that nasty earthquake. Except for this provincial little cabin. But it's hardly the place to raise a child."

"Our home is being rebuilt. You know that."

"But who knows how long it will take? Meanwhile, you and Barbara are living apart. Separated. And she's spending an awful lot of time with that old boyfriend of hers. What's his name? Trent something? Not a good arrangement for a young child."

Barbara stiffened. "Are you suggesting there's something improper going on between Trent and me?"

"Now, Barb, I didn't say—"

"He's just a friend. He lost his wife and needs someone to talk to now and then. Doug knows that and he has no problem with Trent. Tell her, Doug."

Barbara noticed that her husband hesitated for just a second before answering. "Barbara's right. I trust her. For you to insinuate that anything is going on between her and Trent is a new low, even for you, Pam."

Pam waved her hand breezily. "All right, I'm sorry. Maybe I'm wrong. Even so, Janee needs a stable home with two parents."

"And that's exactly what she's going to get," said Doug, his tone barely civil.

Pam flashed a cunning little smile. "Well, at least we agree on that."

Benny set down his coffee cup and stood up.

"Listen, babykins, we'd better get going or we'll miss our return flight."

Pam stood and smoothed out her gray gabardine skirt. "You're right, Benny. It's getting dark, and I think we've said all we need to say." She gazed over at Doug and made an exaggeratedly sad face. "Well, brother dear, I guess the next time we see you will be in court. I'm sorry it has to be this way."

"Me, too," said Doug, his lips tight against his teeth.

Pam blew him a kiss, which he ignored.

"Be sure and bring the kid with you when you come to San Francisco," said Benny. "We don't want to make another trip up these wretched mountains to get her."

Pam paused at the doorway. "Wait a minute, Benny. I just want to go and give the little tyke a good-night kiss." Pam tossed Barbara a calculating glance. "After all, we want Janee to know how much we love her. You don't mind, do you, Barb?"

Barbara crossed her arms tightly on her chest. She forced herself to say, "Sure. Go say good-night to Janee. I promised her I'd be in, too."

Pam's stacked heels made a clacking sound on the wood floor as she strutted down the hall. Barbara debated whether to follow Pam to Janee's room, then thought better of the idea. Pam would only accuse her of spying or intruding.

Less than a minute later, Pam burst into the living

room, her face white. "Benny, she's gone. Janee's gone!"

"Gone? What are you talking about?" barked Benny.

"She's not there. Her bed is empty."

"You must have gone to our room by mistake," said Barbara.

"I know a child's room from a master bedroom," said Pam thickly. "I'm telling you, Janee's not in her bed."

"Then she's probably in the bathroom," said Doug. "Or maybe she went and crawled into our bed."

"No, I checked everywhere. She's not here. Maybe someone's kidnapped her. Do something. Call the police."

Icy alarm prickled Barbara's skin. Pam's concern sounded genuine. "I'll go look." Barbara was already striding down the hall. Her heart hammered as she opened Janee's door and scoured the room with her gaze. There was no sign of Janee. She looked in the bathroom, then crossed the hall to the master bedroom. No Janee.

Doug was close on her heels. "I'll check the closets."

Within minutes they had checked every nook and cranny of the cabin. Barbara's heart thundered in her chest. "Where could she be, Doug? She was just here."

He slipped his arm around her and led her over

to the rocker by the fireplace. "She's got to be close by, Barb. We would have heard if someone had entered the house. The windows are locked. She must have wandered off somehow."

"But where? And why?"

"I smell a rat," said Benny, his eyes narrowing. "Maybe you two had this planned all along. Hide Janee somewhere so we can't get custody."

"Oh, Benny, shut up," said Pam. "My brother wouldn't do some lowlife thing like that. Look at them. They're scared silly."

Benny held up his hands placatingly. "Okay, it was just an idea."

"Benny, if this weren't a crisis situation," said Doug hotly, "I'd show you what I think of your ideas." He strode off down the hall and was back moments later. "I checked the back door again. It's slightly ajar. Janee must have gone outside."

"Or someone came in," said Barbara with a shudder.

"I'm going to check around the yard. She might just be outside looking for pinecones or something."

"Well, I'm calling the police," said Pam, picking up the phone.

"Do that," said Barbara. "Doug and I will be outside." Then she paused as a horrifying thought struck. "What if she ran away?"

Doug frowned. "Why would she do that?"

Barbara clasped her hand over her mouth, comprehension striking like a lightning bolt. "Oh, Doug, maybe she overheard our conversation."

"What conversation?"

"Remember, she peeked around the corner, and we told her to get back to bed? What if she heard Pam saying we didn't want her and would never love her? I can't bear to think of it."

"But she wouldn't run away."

"Wouldn't she?"

Pam hung up the phone. "The police are on their way."

"I'm not waiting for the police," said Doug, grabbing his jacket and a flashlight.

Barbara slipped on her windbreaker and followed him outside. It was dark now, the air brisk, the October wind biting. "She doesn't even have her coat, Doug. Just her flannel shirt and dungarees."

"She can't have gone far, Barb. We'll find her."

Barbara's hopes swelled as she thought of a possibility. "Maybe she ran over to Trent's cabin. She's crazy about him. Maybe she went to say hello."

"Let's check."

To Barbara's disappointment, Janee hadn't ventured over to the next cabin, but Trent quickly offered to join the search. "First, I'll make a few calls," he said, seizing his cell phone. "There are lots of folks on the mountain who would want to help look for her."

"We'll search the woods behind our cabin," said Doug. "Trent, you cover your property."

"Will do."

They had just begun exploring the backyard when Barbara heard a siren. "The police are here, Doug."

"We'd better go back to the house and talk to them. No telling what Pam and Benny will say."

They spent several precious minutes—time they could have spent searching for Janee—answering the officers' endless questions. Had Janee wandered off before? Was she upset about something? Had they noticed any strangers prowling around? On and on. Finally, in exasperation, Barbara said, "Sergeant, we've told you everything we know. Can't you just go look for her?"

"Ma'am, we already have officers out combing the area. If she's out there, we'll find her."

"We're going to look, too," said Doug, "so if there are no more questions—"

"Let the professionals handle this, Dr. Logan," said the officer. "We'd rather have you folks stay close to home—in case the child returns."

"We'll stay close by," said Doug, "but we're still going to take a look around."

Doug got another flashlight for Barbara, and they went outside. Hand in hand they walked around the yard, first the front, then thc side and the back, calling Janee's name, then listening for a little girl's voice amid the sounds of the night.

"Doug, where could she have gone?"

"Almost anywhere."

"She could catch her death of cold. Or a coyote could attack her. She could fall..."

"Don't anticipate the worst, Barb. We've got to believe she's okay."

After searching the yard, they ventured into the woods, following a narrow path through brambles and twigs. "We promised the police we wouldn't go far away," Barbara reminded Doug, as he held back a branch for her.

"I know, but I can't sit and twiddle my thumbs. We have to keep looking."

They followed one path through the spiky pines, then another, calling Janee's name over and over. After a while, Barbara stopped and sat down on a boulder jutting out from a small thicket. Doug sat down beside her and held her close. "You're cold."

"A little. And weary. I need a minute to catch my breath." She gazed up at the patches of sky glimmering through the dense pine fronds. The moon was full, its light smudged by wisps of clouds. A breeze stirred, rustling dry leaves and whispering through the fanning branches. "Do you see the face in the moon, Doug?" she murmured. "When I was a little girl, I thought it was the face of God smiling down on me. I loved a full moon because it made God seem so close."

Doug coughed uneasily. "I'm afraid I haven't thought much about God for a long time. Except when we're in church."

Barbara gazed up at her husband. There in the

moonlight he had never looked more stalwart and handsome. "I was angry at God after Caitlin died," she confessed. "I closed my heart to Him."

Doug nodded. "I know."

"I closed my heart to you, too, Doug," she said in a small, penitent voice.

"I know, Barbie."

"I didn't mean to, Doug. I just felt numb. It was as if everything inside me closed up and shut down. My emotions wouldn't work anymore. I couldn't feel anything."

Doug's voice was solemn. "I know. You couldn't help it."

"Is that why you threw yourself into your work? Because I wasn't there for you?"

He shrugged. "I don't know, Barb. I guess I figured you didn't love me the same way anymore. I knew you blamed me for Caitlin's death. But you had a right. I blamed myself."

She stared up at him. "Blamed you? What are you talking about? Why would I blame you?"

His voice grew heavy with emotion. "I'm a doctor. I'm supposed to be able to help people, make them well. But I couldn't save my own daughter."

"It wasn't your fault, Doug."

"Wasn't it? I let her ride her bike without her helmet. And when the doctors said she was well enough to go home, I didn't argue. I went along. But in the pit of my stomach I knew she shouldn't go home yet. I took her anyway because they said she was ready. Maybe I didn't want to look like an overprotective dad to my colleagues—I don't know."

"You couldn't have known about the blood clot. No one could have known. It would have happened even if she'd been in the hospital."

"I know the facts, Barb. I know them in my head, and everything you say is true. But I can't feel them in my heart. All I feel is the guilt. I hear the recriminations in my head over and over, every day."

"Oh, Doug, is that why you gave up your surgical practice? Is that why you became a hospital administrator, instead?"

"I suppose that was a large part of it."

Barbara clasped Doug's hand and pressed his sturdy fingers against her lips. "I had no idea you felt that way. You never should have given up your medical career. You're wrong to blame yourself."

"Why? It's how you feel, too. I know it is. I've read it in your eyes every day for four years."

She leaned her head against his warm cheek. "I don't blame you, Doug. At least, I don't think I do. Lately my feelings are so jumbled, I don't know what I feel."

Doug was silent for a long time. Finally he said in a voice that was barely audible, "Barbie, I killed your love as surely as I killed Caitlin. If I'd been a better doctor, a better husband, a better father—"

She silenced him with a finger to his lips. "Don't say that, Doug. It's not true. If I made you feel that way, I'm sorry. You must know I never stopped loving you."

"But you never wanted to make love after Caitlin died."

"Not because I didn't love you, Doug. Because somehow it seemed wrong to take pleasure in the very act that had created Caitlin. I couldn't let myself feel pleasure because then I'd feel the pain, too."

"I only wanted to be close to you, to comfort you."

"I needed another kind of comfort, Doug. I needed you to tell me how you felt. I needed you to weep with me over Caitlin, but after that first day, you never cried again. I couldn't understand how you could just pick up your life and go on without ever shedding another tear."

"I didn't want to upset you."

"I longed for us to weep together. I felt as if our relationship had become a barren desert that only our tears could water. But you never offered them."

"I never knew, Barb. I'm sorry."

"I'm sorry, too. Sorry I closed you out and made you think I blamed you. I never did."

"Are you sure?"

"Right now, I'm not sure of anything, except that I love you."

He held her tightly against him. "I love you, too."

They slipped into a pensive silence again. Finally

Barbara said, "Maybe a part of me did blame you, Doug. I blamed God. I closed my heart to Him just as I closed myself to you. But these last few weeks I've begun to find Him again, and He's healing me. Really healing me from the inside out. I feel love blossoming in my heart again—love for you, love for God, love for Janee—replacing the numbness and the anger. I know—and this is hard to say—but I know His love will sustain us, no matter what happens with Janee."

"You make me hungry for that kind of faith, Barb."

"It's not me, Doug. It's what God has done in my heart. It's all Him."

"I wish I had that kind of closeness with Him. It's been a long, dry spell trying to make it on my own."

"We could pray now, Doug. Please. Pray for Janee. Pray for us."

"I'm rusty. I don't know the words."

"Say what's in your heart."

Doug squeezed Barbara's hand tightly, lowered his head and said falteringly, "God, I'm not good at this…finding the right words…saying what I feel. You and I—we've been out of touch too long. Help me make things right with You—and right with Barb. Help us to find Janee. And if You're willing, we'd sure like a chance to raise her as our own. Thanks, Lord, for listening."

"Yes, Lord, thank you," Barbara whispered. She

relaxed her forehead against Doug's cheek and marveled to find it wet with tears. "Doug, you're crying."

Embarrassed, he drew back and with an awkward hand wiped away the wetness. "No, I'm just a little choked up," he conceded.

She seized his hand and touched the velvety smooth cheek where the tears had been. "Don't brush them away, darling. I've waited too long for them. Those tears are watering the garden of our love." She nuzzled her cheek against his and whispered, "And our prayers are the sunshine making our love grow again, because we have the Son shining in our hearts."

He chuckled. "We could wax poetic all night, Barbie, but we'd better get back to the cabin and see if they've found Janee."

She stood up, still holding his hand. "Oh, Doug, I pray to God they've found her."

In less than ten minutes they arrived back at the cabin. As they made their way through the dusky backyard toward the house, Barbara spotted someone moving through the shadows. It was Trent Townsend crossing his property toward them with something in his arms. As he approached, Barbara could see more clearly. Dear heavens, Janee!

Was she alive? Hurt?

Barbara broke into a run toward them, Doug swiftly on her heels. "Janee! Janee!" she cried as she closed the distance between the two yards. She was breathing hard when she reached Trent. Even in the chill air she felt feverish with anxiety and excitement.

"I found our girl, Barb," Trent trumpeted proudly.

Barbara was panting, holding her aching sides as she searched Janee's moonlit face. "Are—Are you okay, baby?"

Trent hoisted Janee up against his broad shoulder. "She's fine, Barb. A little scared."

Janee's corn-silk hair was mussed, and dirt smudged her round cheeks. Her lower lip stuck out in a pout as she wound her arms tightly around Trent's neck.

"Where was she?" asked Doug, joining them.

"In a little alcove at the back of my property. A small cave beside a grassy thicket in the woods."

"A cave?" Barbara echoed uncomprehendingly.

"Yeah, a cave. Hardly more than a hollow in the rock. She was curled up asleep like a little snail."

"How would she find a cave?"

"Janee and I discovered it that day we were putting out the nesting boxes, Barbara. Janee was fascinated by it. She was sure it was the home of some cute little animal."

"Yes, I think she might have mentioned it." Barbara held her arms out to Janee. "Come here, sweetie. I'm so glad Trent found you. We were so worried."

Janee gazed solemnly at Barbara for a moment,

then turned away, burrowing her face against Trent's shoulder.

Barbara exchanged a puzzled glance with Doug, then tried again. "Please, Janee, talk to me. I love you, honey."

Janee peered around at Barbara with dark, reproachful eyes. "You want your other little girl," she said in a small, accusing voice. "Not me. She's the one you love."

Barbara reeled, stricken, Janee's anguished words piercing her heart. Heaven help her, Janee had heard Pam's dark accusations! With tears blinding her eyes Barbara reached out instinctively for Janee, and the child reluctantly allowed herself to be gathered into Barbara's arms. She was a wonderful bundle of paradoxes—a cuddly warm body, cold arms, wet cheeks, and hair filled with the sweet smells of the forest and night air.

Barbara held her close and smoothed her tousled curls. "Janee, darling, don't you understand? I love you both. You and Caitlin. Just like you still love your mommy in heaven. But that's okay. Because our hearts are big enough to hold lots of love."

Janee's lower lip trembled. "But Aunt Pam said you don't want me. She said you wanted me to go away."

"That's not true, Janee. I want you to stay. I love you so much, I want you to be my own little girl."

Doug came over and circled them both in his

strong, warm arms and said, "We both want you to be our little girl, Janee."

She looked up, from one to the other, her tearful eyes full of bright expectancy. "Forever and always?"

"Forever and always, darling." But even as Barbara said the words, a chill of apprehension swept through her. She had made a promise she wasn't sure she could keep. A judge in a courtroom in San Francisco would decide whose little girl Janee would be. In a few short words—with the implacable power of the law behind him and the ear-splitting pounding of his gavel—he could wrench Janee from their arms forever.

How could she possibly make him see how much she and Doug needed this child?

Chapter Fifteen

The sprawling, high-ceilinged room with its stiff mahogany benches and its wide towering desk flanked by American flags looked like a stage set out of an old TV courtroom drama. Barbara realized she had never actually seen a courtroom, except on television. This one had a slightly musty, imposing aura, the smell of yellowing history texts, the dour solemnity of a judge.

Judge Barry Wetherell was a bald, stodgy man in his mid-sixties whose flowing black robe didn't quite hide his enormous girth. His thick-jowled face seemed frozen in a perpetual frown. His small eyes were as cold and hard as steel ball bearings. Barbara had a sinking feeling she would never be able to squeeze an ounce of compassion out of this stern, iron-faced man.

"I don't think we have a prayer," she whispered

to Doug, sitting beside her. Their attorney, Randolph Tate, and the Cotters' lawyer had been summoned to the bench and were discussing something in hushed, sober voices with the equally sober-faced judge.

"Don't say we don't have a prayer, Barb," replied Doug. "All we have is a prayer. And God willing, that's enough."

Barbara glanced over at Pam and Benny, sitting stonily across from them and looking infuriatingly smug. "I pray you're right, Doug, but I have this terrible premonition we're going to face the fight of our lives today."

He squeezed her hand. "At least we're facing it together."

She managed a wobbly smile. "Whatever happens, we have each other. And the Lord."

Doug nodded. "Don't worry, Barbie. God didn't bring us this far to let us down."

Judge Wetherell sat back and pounded his gavel. "Mr. and Mrs. Cotter and Dr. and Mrs. Logan, I've conferred with your attorneys, and if the four of you are in agreement, I'd like to suggest that we attempt to settle this custody matter in my chambers. After all, this isn't a criminal case, and we're not trying to determine innocence or guilt. You're two nice families who want what's best for your niece, and you need my help in making that decision. I think a comfortable, nonthreatening setting will facilitate matters. So I've suggested that your attorneys postpone their arguments until we've had a chance to visit informally. Any objection?"

"No, Your Honor," said Doug.

"Wait a minute, Judge," said Benny. "You want us to hash this out without our lawyers present? I'm not so sure that's a good idea." He cast a suspicious glance at Doug and Barbara. "How do we know they won't pull something?"

Judge Wetherell sat forward, his arms folded on the desk. "You don't trust your brother- and sister-in-law, Mr. Cotter?"

"I didn't say that, Judge."

"Well, if you prefer, Mr. Cotter, we can continue with the hearing here in the courtroom, with your attorney presenting your case."

Barbara rolled her eyes at Doug. As they'd anticipated, Benny was going to do his best to make things complicated. He wouldn't be happy until he'd dragged the whole family through the wringer. Hadn't they all endured enough pain already?

Pam spoke up suddenly, her voice bright and brittle. "Wait a minute, Judge. What my husband Benny is trying to say is, we'd be pleased to settle this in your chambers. Like you said, we're all family."

"Fine, Mrs. Cotter. Then let's adjourn to my chambers."

Barbara gave a sigh of relief.

The judge's chambers was infinitely less intimidating than the courtroom. Two walls were lined with bookcases and the other two displayed ornately framed paintings—familiar prints from the Old Masters. The room was elegant, yet still comfortable and inviting with its heavy oak furniture and black leather chairs. Barbara and Doug sat down without a glance at Pam and Benny, and they all waited in silence as Judge Wetherell bustled in and settled into the chair behind his massive desk.

"Now, this is better, isn't it?" he said, adjusting his robes and flashing the slightest hint of a smile.

Barbara returned a restrained half smile. Maybe the man wasn't going to be such an unfeeling tyrant, after all.

Benny sat forward and rapped his thick knuckles on the judge's desk. "The thing is, Judge, Pam and I were the first ones to petition the court to adopt our little niece, and we think our request should be honored."

"Benny's right," said Pam, smoothing her cranberry-red, knit chemise skirt over her crossed knees. "It's a simple cut-and-dried case. We want the child and we have the most to offer her."

"You may assume that to be true, Mrs. Cotter, but—"

"It's true, Your Honor. My own sister-in-law begged us to take Janee, and now that we're trying to do just that, she and my brother are all up in arms. It's like they don't want her, but they don't want us to have her, either."

"That's a bald-faced lie," countered Doug.

"What kind of sister are you, Pam, lying through your—"

"It's no lie, Doug. The truth is, I'm trying to protect our niece from your neurotic, unstable wife!"

Barbara recoiled, stunned. "Pam, how could you—?"

Doug's face flamed with indignation. "Are you out of your mind, Pam? My wife is the most grounded, centered person I know! And she loves Janee as much as I do!"

"Yes, this week maybe, but what about next week?"

Judge Wetherell banged his palm on the desktop. "Mr. and Mrs. Cotter, Dr. and Mrs. Logan, if you continue this bickering among yourselves, we'll return to the courtroom and let your attorneys battle this out. But, believe me, it bodes best for all of you if we settle this here in a calm, congenial manner. Are you agreed?" He paused for a moment, silently acknowledging their nods, then cleared his throat noisily. "You will each have a chance to have your say—*without* interruption. Is that understood? Now, Mr. Cotter, you seem the most eager to speak out, so why don't you begin?"

"Thank you, Judge." Benny straightened his shoulders and cast a sidelong glance in Doug and Barbara's direction. Barbara met his gaze unflinchingly, mentally daring him to try anything unethical. After all, this wasn't Benny's used car lot, and the judge wasn't some naive, unsuspecting customer.

"It's like this, Judge. My wife and I never had kids. We wanted them, but it just never happened, you know? We weren't blessed that way. Then when Pam's sister died—God rest her soul—well, we figured maybe this was our chance to give this poor orphaned child—our own flesh and blood, mind you—a taste of the good life.

"You see, Pam's sister Nancy was one of those bohemian, earth-mother types, a leftover from the hippie movement. A gypsy at heart. Free-spirited. A plain, simple life-style. No frills. Well, if that was the way she wanted to raise her daughter, who were we to object? But after Paul and Nancy died, Pam and I says to ourselves, hey, we can give this child the kind of life a kid only dreams of. A big house. Fancy clothes. The best schools. Culture. A real high-society life, if she wants it. Anything her little heart desires."

Barbara looked at Doug and shook her head. Benny was laying it on thick. Was the judge buying it? she wondered.

"Mr. Cotter, according to the records I have before me, your sister-in-law, Nancy Myers, appointed her brother and his wife, Dr. and Mrs. Logan, the child's legal guardians. Why should the court overrule Mrs. Myers's instructions and allow you and your wife to adopt her daughter?"

"That's easy, Judge. Nancy picked her brother because she felt sorry for him and Barbara. Their daughter died a few years back. I think Nancy figured if something happened to her, her little girl Janee would make up for Barb and Doug's loss. Only that's not how it worked out."

"Would you like to explain that observation, Mr. Cotter?"

"Sure, Judge." Benny's corpulent face reddened and he shifted his gaze slightly, as if uncomfortable with what he was about to say. "The thing is, Judge—and this isn't easy to say, as fond as I am of my brother- and sister-in-law—they've got serious problems. Problems a poor orphan kid doesn't need."

"Problems?" repeated Judge Wetherell. "Would you be more specific, Mr. Cotter?"

Benny loosened his red paisley tie. "It's like this, Judge. Barbara and Doug never got over losing their kid. It did something to them, you know? It's like they stopped living, stopped having any fun, like they shriveled up and died, too. At first we figured having Janee would be good for them. You know, bring a little life back into their home and give them some happiness again. But the whole thing backfired. I tell you, it was a royal disaster. After a few weeks Barbara phoned Pam and begged her to take Janee off her hands. She said the child hated her, and she couldn't stand to have the girl in her home anymore. I'll tell you the truth, Barbara sounded like she was having a nervous breakdown." Benny looked at his wife. "Didn't she, Pam? Sounded like she was coming unglued, right?"

Pam sat forward eagerly, her slim, crossed legs remaining perfectly poised. "That's right, Judge. You should have heard poor Barbara. She was beside herself, going to pieces..."

Barbara listened, clenching her fists until her nails dug into her palms. Pam's words were searing. Barbara fought every nerve in her body to keep from jumping up and speaking out—putting Pam and Benny in their place. Leaning over to Doug, she whispered, "Can't we do something? She's making me sound like a psychological basket case!"

He clasped her hand. "Hold tight, Barb. We'll have our turn."

"Like Benny says, Barbara sounded so desperate, we didn't know what she might do," Pam continued with mock sympathy.

"Please, Mrs. Cotter," intoned the judge. "You'll have your chance to speak shortly." He looked back at Benny. "So, Mr. Cotter, did you and your wife take the child at that time?"

"No, not then, Judge. Pam and I were having a few problems of our own at the time. Nothing serious, mind you. Just some financial matters we had to work out. But once we knew Doug and Barbara didn't want the child, we started making plans to adopt her ourselves. I mean, it was the only way. We could see the arrangement with Barb and Doug and the kid was deteriorating fast.

"And, of course, right after Barbara called Pam, they had the big earthquake in Los Angeles and their house was damaged. So they couldn't even provide a home for the kid anymore. They took her up to some lonely old cabin in the woods and kept her there."

"I see from my notes that you must be speaking of their mountain home at Lake Arrowhead?"

"Yes, Your Honor."

Judge Wetherell's lips curled ironically. "Lonely old cabin, is it? I've been to Lake Arrowhead, and most of the homes there are quite adequate."

"Sure, it's an okay place, but not to raise a kid."

"Mr. Cotter, let's focus on your own personal reasons for wanting to adopt your niece."

Benny shrugged. "Like I said, she's a nice kid. She needs a stable home with two parents who want her, who aren't carrying around a lot of emotional baggage from the past. That's us—Pam and me. We love the little tyke. She had a great time while she was staying with us. Just ask her. She had a blast."

Judge Wetherell tapped his fingertips on his desk and turned to Pam. "Mrs. Cotter, what would you like the court to know about your petition to adopt your young niece, Janee Myers?"

Pam uncrossed her long legs and sat forward with an urgent conspiratorial air. "Judge Wetherell," she said in her most animated voice, "I don't know if I can add anything to what my husband's told you, except that we want very much to raise our little niece. As Benny said, she won't want for a thing. Benny is a very successful businessman, and I work with him, keeping his books, so I'll be home with Janee most of the time. I assure you it'll be an ideal arrangement."

"I appreciate your confidence, Mrs. Cotter. Is that all?"

"No, Your Honor." Pam fluffed her ebony, perfectly coiffed hair and cast a cryptic glance at Doug and Barbara. "There's much more, Your Honor."

Judge Wetherell heaved a patient sigh. "I'm listening, Mrs. Cotter."

Pam lifted her chin jauntily. "Your Honor, it isn't just that I believe Benny and I would be the best parents for Janee. I'm convinced it would be a tragedy for my brother and his wife to adopt her."

"A tragedy?" echoed Barbara incredulously. She turned to Doug. "Is she crazy? What is she talking about?"

"Mrs. Logan, please," Judge Wetherell admonished. "You'll have your chance to speak later."

"Thank you, Your Honor," Pam said in her honey-coated voice. "You see, even though my brother and sister-in-law were made Janee's legal guardians, they never made the slightest effort to adopt Janee until they found out we wanted her. If you ask me, I think they're behaving like spoilsports."

"That may be your opinion, Mrs. Cotter, but that doesn't constitute a tragedy in my book."

"I was just getting to that, Your Honor," Pam rushed on. "As much as I hate to say it, I'm convinced that Barbara is not emotionally equipped to raise this child.''

''Would you like to explain yourself, Mrs. Cotter?''

''Yes, I would. The fact is, my sister-in-law doesn't know what true commitment means.''

''That's not true, Pam!'' countered Barbara hotly, nearly bolting from her chair.

''Sit down, Mrs. Logan,'' urged the judge.

Pam swiveled in her chair and gazed coldly at Barbara. ''For crying out loud, Barb, you're virtually separated from my brother. The two of you aren't even living under the same roof anymore. What kind of marriage is that?''

Barbara shook her head, her mind reeling, tears welling in her eyes. ''How can you even ask that, Pam?''

''And, what's worse, you've taken up with that old boyfriend of yours in the mountains. Wasn't he the love of your life, Barb, the man you never got over?''

Doug sprang from his chair. ''That's enough, Pam! You're out of line.''

Pam forged ahead heedlessly. ''How convenient that Trent Townsend lives right next door to you, Barb. But that hardly matters, because when Benny and I came to visit we found your handsome Mr. Townsend right there in your cozy little cabin with you and Janee. No wonder you don't want to go home to Doug.''

"How dare you, Pam! How could you!" Barbara felt herself collapsing inside, her emotions unraveling. She was swooning, sinking. "You're twisting everything!" She reached out for Doug, and he gripped her hand.

Pam remained unruffled. "I'm sorry, Barb. I've been silent long enough. You tell me—what kind of message does that send to an innocent child? You and your old boyfriend shacking up in your little mountain hideaway?"

"We never—Trent's a friend, nothing more." Barbara stared at her husband. She was trembling, cotton-mouthed. "You believe me, don't you, Doug?"

Judge Wetherell broke in. "Mrs. Logan, Mrs. Cotter, I will not have this hearing deteriorate into name-calling and hysterics. If we can't resolve this situation calmly and with decorum, I'll place the child in a foster home until the court can decide where she belongs."

The judge fixed his gaze on Pam. "You may continue, but I order you to discuss only the child, not idle rumors and hearsay."

Pam shrugged and settled back in her chair. "Whatever you say, Judge Wetherell. But I want you to understand. I'm not trying to besmirch my sister-in-law's good name. It's just that I can't figure her out. One minute she's begging me to take Janee, and then she's saying she wants to keep her. So which is it?"

"You know which it is, Pam," said Barbara under her breath.

"Where is this conversation headed, Mrs. Cotter?"

"Just this, Your Honor." Pam licked her glossy lips and inhaled deeply, as if she were gearing up for a new verbal attack. "Personally—and I say this with deep concern—I think Barbara has an unhealthy fixation on Janee. She sees her as the little girl she lost."

"I do not, Pam! You know I—"

Pam pivoted, legs crossed again, and looked directly at Barbara with her cool, violet-gray eyes. "I'm sorry, Barb. I've got to say it. You're trying to replace your dead child with Janee. But it won't work. Janee isn't Caitlin, and if you tried to raise her, one of these days you'd realize that and want us to take Janee away. Just like you did when you phoned me that day."

"You'll never let me live down that call, will you!"

"Why should I, Barb? You can't do that to Janee again. She's been through too much already. You know I'm right. If you care about her, do what's best for Janee and let us take her."

A sob tightened Barbara's throat. Her head ached, her senses whirled. She couldn't think, couldn't speak, couldn't ward off any more of Pam's vocal blows or deflect her vile arguments. Maybe it was all true. Maybe on some subconscious level she had encouraged Trent's affection. Maybe she was trying to replace her darling Caitlin with little Janee. Was she so blind to her own motives that she couldn't even see what she was doing?

Surely she was committed totally to her marriage and to Doug. Surely she wanted Janee for her own sake. Didn't she?

"Barbara, honey, are you okay?" Doug was leaning close, gripping her arm, looking concerned. "Barb, do you hear me?"

She wanted to respond, but a paralysis had seized her body even as emotions rose in her chest and pressed painfully against her ribs.

Judge Wetherell was watching her intently, his small black eyes narrowing in small pouches of flesh. "Mrs. Logan, are you ill?"

She managed to shake her head.

"Would you like some water?"

"No."

"Are you able to tell the court your side of the story?"

Barbara closed her eyes and covered her mouth with her hand. God help her, she was falling apart at the most crucial moment of her life and coming across as an emotional wreck.

"Your Honor, maybe I should speak first," said Doug, still holding her arm protectively.

"I have a better idea, Dr. Logan," said Judge Wetherell. "Let's adjourn for the day. We'll reconvene in the morning. My chambers. Nine a.m." He pushed back his chair, then paused and looked at Doug. "Before you go...where's the child, our little Janee Myers? Did she come to San Francisco with you?"

"Yes," said Doug. "She's at our hotel. With a sitter the hotel provides."

The judge rubbed his chin, contemplating something. "I'll tell you what, Dr. and Mrs. Logan. I'd like you to bring the child with you tomorrow. I want to have a little talk with her myself."

Doug's tone was guarded. "Is that necessary?"

"Yes, Dr. Logan. I think it is. I have a feeling a little conversation with Janee might be very enlightening. Just what the court needs in making its decision."

That evening, during their drive back to the hotel, Barbara looked desolately at Doug and said, "We've lost her, haven't we? The judge is going to let Pam and Benny adopt Janee."

Doug kept his gaze on the road. "We don't know that for sure, Barb."

"I know it, Doug. I feel it in every fiber of my bones. There's nothing we can say tomorrow to counteract all the venom Pam and Benny spewed."

"Stop it, Barb. We can't let ourselves give up. The judge will hear our side in the morning. He'll see that we're the ones who should have Janee."

"Will he?" said Barbara darkly. Her voice broke with unexpected anguish. "How do we know Pam's not right about me, Doug?"

He stared at her. "What are you talking about, Barb?"

"Can you believe it?" she said shakily. "Pam's got me doubting myself, Doug, questioning my own motives. I don't know what's true anymore."

"Don't pay any attention to her, Barb. My sister's a cunning, mean-spirited woman. She had no right to say those things."

"What if Pam's right? What if I'm not right for Janee? What if I'm destined to be a failure as a wife and a mother?"

Doug reached across the seat for her hand. "Don't do this to yourself, Barb. Please. We've got to believe everything will turn out for the best."

She shuddered inwardly. How could she make him comprehend the knot of cold, hard fear in the pit of her stomach? "The only thing I'm certain of right now, Doug, is that we're not going to get to take our little girl home with us."

Chapter Sixteen

When they arrived back at the hotel on Fisherman's Wharf, Doug parked their rental car in the parking structure, but instead of getting out, he turned in his seat to face Barbara. "Listen, honey, before we go in, let's talk a minute."

"Here in the car? Why not inside?"

"Because Janee's there in the suite with the sitter. We need to settle a few things privately first."

Her heart sank. "Don't tell me you're starting to believe the things Pam said about me, too."

He took both her hands in his. His grip was warm, firm. His sturdy face was semi-obscured by evening shadows, but he was still the most handsome man she had ever known. And the most wonderful. She couldn't stand to lose him now.

"Are you serious, Barb? I don't believe a word Pam said, but I can see that her words have eaten away at your self-confidence. You're listening to the wrong voice, honey."

"The wrong voice?"

He drew closer to her, massaging her shoulder with one firm hand. The spicy fragrance of his aftershave scented the air. "Barb, you're the one who's taught me so much lately about faith," he said softly, his voice tender, consoling. "About our walk with God. You made me realize we've got to keep our eyes focused on Christ, always, every moment of every day. It's the only way to survive this life. If we focus on ourselves, we get discouraged because we see only frail, fallible human beings. If we focus on our circumstances, we feel hopeless and overwhelmed because we see all the problems and troubles on every side. But when we look to the Lord, we see all-encompassing power and unconditional love. We can do all things through Christ, Barb. He promises us that. We can win Janee. Or we can survive without her...through Christ. We have Him. We have each other. That's all that matters."

Barbara went into her husband's arms and savored his warm, solid strength and closeness. "Oh, Doug, I love you. Thank you for reminding me of God's love...and yours. And thank you for reminding me why I love you so much."

"I'm getting pretty good at this prayer business, Barb," he murmured against her ear. "Shall we take a few minutes now and turn over all our concerns to God?''

Barbara burrowed her head in the curve of his neck. ''Please, darling. You begin, and I'll follow.''

Later, as Barb and Doug took the elevator up to their second-floor hotel suite, she felt as if she'd been given back her life. The poison of Pam's words had been washed away by the deep, utter conviction that God loved her and would give her His best always. In that truth she could rest, no matter what happened.

As soon as they entered their suite, Janee came bounding into their arms. ''Aunt Barbara, can we go home on the big airplane now? Can we go back to our cabin in the mountains?''

Barbara squeezed Janee in her arms, treasuring her sweet warmth. ''Not yet, honey. Maybe tomorrow.''

''Okay, but I can't wait.'' Janee looked over at her sitter, a smiling, middle-aged matron with graying streaks in her permed hair. ''Edith and I were playing Go Fish. It's lots of fun.''

''Sounds great, honey,'' said Doug. He turned to Edith. ''Mrs. Reid, would you mind staying this evening? We're going to take Janee out to dinner, then Barbara and I will be going out for a while.''

''That's fine by me, Dr. Logan. You bring Janee back when you're ready, and I'll get her tucked into bed for you.''

Janee tugged on Doug's arm. "No, I wanna go with you and Aunt Barbara. Please! Please!"

Doug swung her up in his arms. "Listen, half-pint, by the time we get you stuffed with hamburgers and milk shakes, you'll want to come back here and go right to sleep."

"Can I watch TV first?"

"If Mrs. Reid can find you a program worth watching."

"I'll do my best, Dr. Logan."

"Great! Then get your jacket, Janee, and let's go chow down some burgers."

They walked nearly two blocks downhill from the hotel to the harbor, Janee walking between them and holding their hands. From time to time they lifted her high between them and swung her back and forth. Each time she laughed and begged them to do it again.

"Why are all the buildings on hills?" she asked, looking around.

"Because that's how San Francisco is," said Doug.

Janee chuckled. "Everything is up and down, up and down." She watched a trolley trundle by. "Can we ride the funny car?" she begged. "Please, Uncle Doug?"

"Sure. After we eat. We'll take the cable car and go up and down some rib-tickling hills."

Janee looked up quizzically. "Do they really tickle your ribs?"

"You bet. Just wait and see. They tickle you right in the tummy." Doug playfully tickled her middle, and she doubled over in laughter. "But first we've got to get you that hamburger."

"With *this* many French fries." Janee held up ten fingers.

Doug nodded. "And lots of ketchup, right?"

"Right!"

They found a fast-food restaurant a block from the harbor. Doug and Barb sipped soft drinks, while Janee consumed a double cheeseburger, a large order of fries and a chocolate shake.

As Janee slurped the last of her shake, Barbara said with a teasing smile, "After eating all that junk food, you're going to dream of pink elephants."

Doug chuckled. "And not just any pink elephants. They'll be pink elephants dancing in a circle with tutus and flowerpot hats."

"No, I won't dream of elephants," Janee scoffed. "I'll dream of fish."

"Fish?" they echoed in unison.

She gave an exaggerated nod. "Big fish and little fish and fat fish and skinny fish."

"Why fish?" asked Barbara.

Janee held her nose. "Because the air smells like fish. All yucky!"

"That's because we're here at the harbor," said Doug. "There are lots of fish swimming around in the ocean."

Janee looked thoughtful for a moment. "I won't

dream of elephants or fish," she said softly. She looked up with wide, guileless eyes, first at Barbara, then at Doug. "I'm gonna dream that you're my mommy and daddy and I'm your little girl. Forever and always."

Barbara scooped Janee up in her arms—greasy fingers, chocolate-covered face and all. "Sweetie, I pray your dream will come true."

Janee nodded solemnly. "It will, Mommy—I mean, Aunt Barbara. Because I asked Jesus. And you said He hears little girls' prayers."

Sudden tears streamed down Barbara's cheeks. "He does, honey. He loves you even more than we do."

Barbara didn't say much as they walked back to the hotel. She was too choked up and didn't want Janee to see her tears. After tucking a very sleepy youngster into her bed and hearing her muffled prayers, Doug and Barbara said good-night to Mrs. Reid and slipped away quietly.

"Now for some real food," said Doug as they walked hand in hand back downhill to Fisherman's Wharf. "I made reservations for us at that famous fish grotto on the pier overlooking the fishing fleet. It's famous for its Italian seafood and its breathtaking view of the wharf. So are you ready for some shrimp scampi or fresh salmon or lobster tail dipped in drawn butter?"

Barbara tucked her arm in Doug's. "Are you kidding? My mouth is watering already." She gazed around with an invigorating sense of adventure. The cool night air was moist with sea spray, and fog horns echoed across the dark waters. Even at this time of evening the harbor was still bustling with tourists and street vendors, and fishermen docking their boats, and local residents out to sample the cuisine and nightlife at their favorite bistros and clubs.

At the restaurant they were shown to a cozy candlelit table overlooking the wharf. But Barbara found herself too engrossed in her husband to notice the scenery. As they sampled the bread sticks and sipped goblets of sparkling white grape juice, she and Doug sat gazing into each other's eyes like lovesick teenagers.

"You look gorgeous in the candlelight, Barb."

"And you're the same smooth-talking charmer I remember from all those years ago."

He clasped her hand across the linen tablecloth. "You know, it's strange, Barb. In a way I feel like we've been—I don't know how to explain it—frozen in time, numb, in a deep freeze—" A smile played on his lips. "See what I mean? I don't have the right words. But it's as if we're both waking up out of a long sleep and we're finally feeling things again, finally in touch with our emotions. Do you feel it, too?"

"You couldn't have said it better," she agreed. "Tonight I'm feeling emotions I had long forgotten. Sweet, bittersweet, poignant, wonderful emotions.

Love and longing. Wistfulness. Bits of memory...yearnings...and desire."

He kissed her fingertips. "I like the sound of that, sweetheart. Maybe we should skip dinner and go straight to the dessert."

She laughed. "Now that's the old Doug Logan talking."

After dinner they took a long, leisurely stroll in the moonlight along the Embarcadero. They walked arm in arm, locked so close that they moved as one. The pungent sea air was damp and biting, with a sudden wind rising over foamy, crashing waves, but Barbara didn't care. This was a night like none she had ever experienced—a new beginning, imbued with fresh hopes and dreams. She and Doug had found their way back to each other through the darkness. They were alive again, alive in every way. God had brought them healing. And now, this bright magical night, Barbara was aware only of her husband's protective warmth and gentle caress as they laughed and kissed and counted stars and whispered sweet endearments.

All too soon it was time to head back to their hotel. Doug paid Mrs. Reid and sent her on her way, while Barbara showered and slipped into a lacy negligee. Then, while Doug showered, Barbara checked on Janee. She sat down quietly on the bed and gazed at Janee's cherubic face, smoothed back her soft, saffron curls. "I love you, my sweet girl," Barbara whispered. "I just pray that tomorrow you'll be ours, really ours."

Janee stirred and her eyelids fluttered. Her rose-petal lips formed the word, "Mommy."

"God willing," Barbara whispered, tears starting. "Please, God, let it be. You've made me strong, but please don't ask too much of me now."

There was a rustling sound. Barbara looked around, startled. It was Doug joining her at Janee's bedside, loosely tying his velour robe. He nodded at the slumbering child. "She looks like an angel, doesn't she?"

"She is an angel, Doug. Our little angel."

"That's my prayer, Barbie. That she'll be ours."

"My prayer, too."

"He's already answered so many prayers."

"I know, Doug." Barbara rose and slipped into his arms. "He helped us find our way back to each other. I almost wonder if I dare ask for more."

"God's in the business of answering prayers. It's what He does best. I say, go for the moon, if you want it."

"It's not the moon I want, Doug." With an alluring little smile, Barbara ran her fingertips over the solid contours of her husband's chest. "You smell wonderful. What is that? Something new?"

"Something just for you, Barbie." He took her hand and led her quietly to their adjoining room. But just as he was shutting Janee's door, Barbara heard a little voice call out, "Mommy? Daddy? I'm scared."

With muted sighs they both returned to Janee's bedside. Janee sat up and rubbed her eyes with her fists. "I had a bad dream." She looked up at Barbara. "Can I come in bed with you?"

Barbara looked at Doug. "Just for a few minutes?"

He shrugged. "Only until she falls asleep. Then it's just you and me, babe."

"Okay, Janee," said Barbara with a grin. "The big guy says it's okay."

"Oh, boy!" Janee chortled. She jumped out of bed, scampered barefoot from her room to the master suite and dove into the king-size bed. She burrowed down under the covers in the very center and waited for Barbara and Doug to join her, one on each side. When they were all snugly under the covers, Janee whispered, "Look. Three bugs in a rug. Now we're a happy family."

Barbara's throat tightened. *Almost, little one, but not quite.*

Chapter Seventeen

In the car on the way to the courthouse, with Janee chattering happily in the back seat, Barbara felt hopeful about the judge's decision. But as soon as she sat down in Judge Wetherell's chambers and met his steely gaze, she was filled with misgivings. What could she possibly say that would counteract Pam and Benny's destructive words yesterday?

Dear Lord, please help me to keep my eyes focused on You, she prayed silently. *Not on myself or the circumstances. Give me Your strength and show Your love through me. I am Your child and I trust You to do what's best for me...and best for Janee.*

Judge Wetherell broke into her thoughts. "Mrs. Logan, are you ready to address the court today regarding your young niece, Janee Myers?"

Barbara straightened her shoulders and swallowed over the dryness in her throat. "Yes, Your Honor."

The judge sat forward and tented his fingers. "Then please proceed, Mrs. Logan. Tell the court why you believe you and your husband should be allowed to adopt your niece."

Barbara kept her gaze singularly on the judge, not on Pam and Benny. "Your Honor, what my sister-in-law said yesterday was partly true. After Doug and I lost our daughter Caitlin, we both withdrew into ourselves. We erected barriers around our emotions so that we wouldn't have to feel anything. We didn't even know how to comfort each other, so our marriage grew cold. Numbness seemed better than the pain.

"When Janee came into our lives, we were forced to face the truth about ourselves. Doug had buried himself in his work. I was living in the past. We had closed our hearts to each other and to God. Janee forced those doors open and made us feel again. She made us dare to love once more. To love each other. To love another child. To love and trust God again.

"Your Honor, even if you decide we can't have Janee, she's done more for us in the brief time she's been in our lives than anyone else ever could have done. She's given us back everything we thought we'd lost—our love, our hope, our faith."

Barbara's voice caught with sweeping emotion. She drew in a deep breath and steadied herself. *Help me, God. Don't let me falter now.* After a tension-filled silence, she went on with renewed conviction.

"Your Honor, I ask that you let us adopt Janee, because in our hearts she's already ours and we're already hers. We love her as much as any two parents could love a child, and we want what's best for her, just as our Heavenly Father always chooses what's best for us. So whatever you decide today, we know it will be in Janee's best interest and in the providence of God."

The judge drummed his fingers on his desk. "Is there anything else you wish to say, Mrs. Logan?"

Barbara blotted her eyes with a tissue. Her makeup was running, and she probably looked a sight, but it didn't matter. She felt a marvelous peace inside, a certainty that God was in charge and everything would be all right, no matter what happened. "No, Your Honor," she said quietly.

"How about you, Mr. Logan? Would you like to add something to your wife's remarks?"

Doug reached over and clasped Barbara's hand tightly in his. His voice was heavy with feeling. "Only this, Your Honor. I love my wife with all my heart, and I love Janee as if she were my own. God help me, I promise to be the best husband and father I can be."

Judge Wetherell sat back, put on small, wire-rimmed spectacles and folded his robed arms over his ample middle. "Well, then, now I'd like to—"

Benny spoke up, nearly rising from his chair. "Can we say something more, Judge?"

Judge Wetherell peered at Benny over his spectacles. "Mr. Cotter, I think you and Mrs. Cotter had opportunity to convey your opinions yesterday. Do you have something of significance to add to those comments?"

Benny cast an annoyed glance at Doug and Barbara. "No, Judge, I guess I don't have anything more to add."

"Fine, then." Judge Wetherell made a rumbling sound in his throat. "Now I would like to speak privately with young Janee Myers. Where is the girl, Mrs. Logan?"

"She's just outside, putting together a jigsaw puzzle with your bailiff."

"Ah, yes." The judge stifled an amused smile. "Please, send her in as you leave."

"Judge, when will we know your decision?" asked Benny, standing and straightening his yellow paisley sports jacket. "You're not going to make us come back another day, are you? I've got a business to run back in Oregon, you know."

"I'm aware of that, Mr. Cotter. The court will render its decision after I've talked with your niece."

"You know my brother and his wife have probably coached her," said Pam thickly. "I'm sure they've filled her head with all kinds of wild promises."

"Don't worry, Mrs. Cotter. I'm a grandfather. I think I can handle a five-year-old. I'm sure we'll have a very enlightening conversation."

For over half an hour Barbara and Doug sat on a hard bench in the hall outside the courtroom, while Judge Wetherell visited with Janee in his chambers. Pam and Benny sat on a bench some distance away, hurling smoldering glances, refusing even to engage in chitchat.

Finally the bailiff signaled for the four of them to rejoin the judge in his chambers. Judge Wetherell was sitting behind his desk with Janee on his lap. She smiled contentedly as she tore the wrapper off a candy bar and offered the judge a bite.

"No, thank you, Janee," he said with a hefty chuckle. "It's all yours. I'm watching my waistline, you know, and there's an awful lot of it to watch."

As everyone sat down, the judge shuffled several papers on his desk while still balancing Janee on his knee. As the tension in the room mounted, he cleared his throat loudly and said, "The young lady and I have had a very nice visit. I've learned all about her little stuffed friend Zowie and the elegant Mrs. Miniver, and the nesting boxes Janee placed around her mountain cabin for the baby animals."

He paused and smiled at Janee to make sure he had all of his details correct. Janee nodded, and he proceeded. "I've also learned that Janee had a very pleasant visit with her Aunt Pam and Uncle Benny in Oregon. She's very fond of both of you, Mr. and Mrs. Cotter."

"Of course she is," exclaimed Pam, pleased.

Barbara and Doug exchanged concerned glances.

What Barbara feared most was happening. The judge had been swayed by their arguments. Could she endure this? Her heart hammered in her chest. Surely everyone could hear. *Please, God, please!*

"Janee has also been very happy staying with her Aunt Barbara and Uncle Doug in their cabin in the mountains," said Judge Wetherell, smiling benevolently at Janee. "They've played lots of games and gone for walks in the woods and fed the squirrels and made pinecone people. She says she has started calling the Logans 'Mommy' and 'Daddy' because they love her the way mommies and daddies love their children."

Barbara reached for Doug's hand. Tears flooded her eyes.

Judge Wetherell's tone turned solemn as he gazed at Pam and Benny. "Mr. and Mrs. Cotter, you made many glowing promises yesterday regarding what you would give Janee if you adopted her. The best schools. A beautiful home. Anything her heart desired. But never did you mention the one most important thing. Love."

Barbara held her breath. The world seemed to stop on its axis, waiting, waiting.

"From what I've witnessed today," Judge Wetherell continued, "Janee is already receiving plenty of that very crucial commodity. From the Logans. They love her and she loves them, and as far as I'm concerned that's the most vital ingredient in any relationship. Therefore, the court finds in favor of

Doug and Barbara Logan. The papers will be drawn up for them to adopt their young niece, Janee Myers. This case is dismissed.''

For Barbara, the next few moments were like something out of a dream. She was vaguely aware of standing and moving in slow motion toward the judge's desk. She was aware of Doug catching her around the waist and saying something, his face beaming with joy and excitement. She was aware of Janee jumping down from the judge's lap and racing toward her, and somehow she and Doug and Janee converging in one delirious hug, the three of them exchanging bushels of kisses and tears and laughter.

After signing the necessary legal documents, Barbara and Doug linked arms, with Janee in the middle, and paraded out of the courthouse, swinging Janee in the air between them, letting her soar in the circle of their love.

Epilogue

One year later

As Barbara gazed up at the huge banner over the open doors of the elaborately decorated hotel ballroom, she swallowed over a growing lump in her throat. She wasn't going to cry. She had promised herself, no tears. But they were coming anyway, unbidden, unstoppable as her eyes moved over the heart-stirring words of the blue-and-gold banner.

Celebrating the Opening of the
Caitlin Logan Memorial Pediatric Wing

Barbara looked at Doug beside her, handsome and debonair in his black tuxedo, a red rose boutonniere in his lapel. He had never looked more proud or more impassioned. Tears glistened in his smoky blue eyes as they did in hers. With a quavering little smile she tucked her arm in his and whispered, "This is the day we've waited for, darling. We're doing the last good thing we can for our daughter."

Doug nodded, a tendon tightening in his sculpted jaw. "Caitlin would have loved knowing that thousands of children will be helped in her name."

"Maybe she does know." One warm tear streamed down Barbara's cheek. "It gives Caitlin's short life a whole new purpose, doesn't it? One that will continue long after we're gone."

"God is good," whispered Doug, patting her hand.

Janee tugged on Barbara's arm. "Mommy, let's go in. The party's already started."

Barbara smiled down at her precious Janee, looking like an angel in her pink taffeta party dress, her golden hair in sun-washed ringlets. "We're going in, sweetie. Right now."

"Can I have some pink punch, Mommy? A big glass? And a big piece of Caitlin's birthday cake?"

"Sure, honey. Only it's not Caitlin's birthday cake."

"Yes, it is, Mommy," Janee insisted. "You said this is Caitlin's party. So it's her cake."

Barbara smiled, waves of emotion rising in her chest. "You're right, baby. It's Caitlin's cake, and you can have all you want."

Doug escorted them through a mingling throng of graceful women in formal sequined gowns and elegant men in tuxedos and dinner jackets. Their destination—the refreshment table overflowing with fancy hors d'oeuvres and exotic delicacies: canapes, buffalo wings, smoked salmon, shrimp cocktail, eggrolls and stuffed mushrooms.

Janee solemnly surveyed the sprawling feast and shook her head in dismay. "I want French fries!"

"I'm sorry, honey," said Doug. "French fries aren't on the menu here."

"Why don't you try an eggroll, sweetie?" suggested Barbara. "Then we'll head over to the dessert table and get you that slice of cake you've been waiting for."

Janee clapped her hands. "Yippee! Get me a piece with lots of yummy frosting, Mommy." She opened her arms wide. "This much!"

"Don't worry, honey. You'll have frosting coming out your ears."

"No, Mommy. In my mouth!"

Barbara laughed. "Right. In your mouth, not ears. What am I thinking of?"

Janee hugged Barbara's arm. "You're funny, Mommy. Isn't she funny, Daddy?"

Doug chuckled and gave Barbara an amused glance. "I'm staying out of this discussion."

Barbara nudged him playfully. "You'd better, if you know what's good for you."

"Oh, I do, believe me."

As they headed for the dessert table, Barbara noticed a familiar face in the crowd. Trent Townsend, of all people. In a white dinner jacket, at that! Spotting Barbara, he made his way over, a willowy redhead on his arm.

"Barbara! I wondered if you'd arrived yet." Trent released the redhead and took Barbara in his arms. He kissed her cheek, then offered Doug his hand. "Hey, ol' man. Thanks for sending me the invitation. How's it going?"

"Not bad. How about you?"

"We just got here," said Barbara breathlessly. "I'm so glad Doug invited you, Trent. It's quite a reception, isn't it?"

"A wonderful occasion, darlin'," Trent agreed. "Everyone in town must be here, including the entire medical staff." He leaned over confidentially to Doug. "But tell me, who's running the hospital?"

Doug chuckled. "I'm not sure."

Trent turned back to Barbara and his voice softened. "I know how much this gala affair means to you and Doug."

"Yes, it's very special." Before she got choked up again, Barbara turned her gaze to the auburn-haired beauty in the green velvet gown and smiled.

"Oh, Barb," said Trent, slipping his arm around the woman, "I'd like you to meet my wife, Valerie. Valerie, this is Barbara Logan and her husband Doug and their daughter, Janee."

As everyone shook hands and exchanged pleasantries, Janee gave Trent a big bear hug. "We missed you, Uncle Trent."

He swept her up in his arms. "Well, I've missed you, too, kiddo. Are you still at the cabin?"

"No, we moved back to the big fancy house. It's all fixed up again. No more cracks from the earthquake. And guess what, Uncle Trent!"

"What is it, sweet stuff?"

"I have the pretty room with all the bears and dolls! It's all mine!"

"That's terrific. I'll have to come visit you sometime."

"Please come, Uncle Trent. You can meet Mrs. Miniver. You'll like her. She's the prettiest bear in the world."

"Well, I'd like to meet her. May I bring Valerie?"

"Sure! She can play with my dolls."

Valerie smiled. "I'd like that, honey."

Trent turned to Doug. "So tell me, are you still in fund-raising? Or are you back doing your thing in the operating room again?"

Doug ran his hand over his curly black hair. "You could say I gave up fund-raising for the surgical suite. It's good to be back where I belong."

"What made you change your mind?"

Doug gave Barbara a knowing glance. "I guess you could say I was listening to the wrong voice for a while—the voice of guilt and fear—when I should have been listening to the affirming voice of God."

Trent grinned. "Yeah, I'm learning to listen to God myself. Valerie makes sure we're in church every Sunday. I'm beginning to understand what Barb meant when she talked about God healing wounded hearts.''

Janee patted Trent's cheek. ''Guess what, Uncle Trent!''

He put his large hand over her small one. ''What is it, sweet pea?''

Janee drew in a deep breath as if preparing to expel all the words in one excited breath. ''I'm going to have a new little baby brother or sister.''

Trent gave Barbara a quizzical smile. ''You're expecting a baby?''

A pleasant flush warmed Barbara's cheeks. ''Yes. In about six months.'' Her hands moved unthinkingly to her slightly swelling middle. ''It's another of God's little miracles.''

Trent set Janee down and pumped Doug's hand. ''Well, congratulations again, ol' man. You've been busier than I thought.''

Doug slipped his arm around Barbara and drew her close. With his free hand he cupped her slender hands resting on her abdomen. ''We're pretty excited,'' he agreed, merriment coloring his voice. ''In fact, all three of us are walking around in the clouds these days. Right, Janee?''

''No, Daddy. I walk around on the ground. See?'' She took several exaggerated steps in her shiny black patent-leather shoes.

''What I mean, honey, is you're thrilled about the baby, too. You're already making plans to teach your baby brother or sister all sorts of stuff. Like how to walk. And swim. And throw a ball. Right?''

Janee hunched her shoulders and rocked back and forth on her heels. ''And I'm going to teach her how to color and make pinecone people and nesting boxes,'' she chimed in with a wide, ear-to-ear grin.

A booming voice from the platform silenced them momentarily. ''Ladies and gentlemen, may I please have your attention!'' Dr. Underwood, the hospital administrator, a slender, silver-haired man, spoke into the crackling microphone. ''Folks, I'd like to have Dr. Douglas Logan come up to the podium and say a few words. As you all know, Dr. Logan is responsible for the hospital's new pediatric wing. It is through his tireless fund-raising efforts that this worthy project has reached fruition. Let's give Dr. Logan a rousing round of applause.''

Amid the applause, Doug gazed down at Barbara, his eyes crinkling with pleasure and a hint of embarrassment. He was still holding her in his arms. ''I guess he means me.''

Barbara smiled adoringly. ''Your public awaits.''

''Then it looks like I'd better get up there. Say a prayer for me, okay?''

''I will. Share your heart, darling. They'll love you...just as I do.''

Doug tightened his embrace and kissed Barbara soundly on the lips. ''I love you, Barbie,'' he whispered into her ear. ''More than you'll ever know.''

She sank into the deep, dusky blue of his eyes. "I love you, too, Doug. With all my heart."

Janee squeezed her way between them. "Me, too, Mommy and Daddy. Let me in! Group hug!"

"Amen! Group hug!" boomed Doug, drawing Janee into their embrace. They hugged tightly, laughing breathlessly. Then Doug took their hands and stepped back with an expansive grin. "Listen, you two, I'm not going up on that stage alone. We're in this together, we're in this for a lifetime, so the three of us are going up there—one of you on each side while I make my speech. Okay?"

"Actually, it'll be the four of us up there," said Barbara, patting her rounded tummy, "but who's counting?"

"She means the baby, Daddy," said Janee, her green eyes dancing, her cheeks blushing pink as rose petals. "Remember? The baby!"

"Are you kidding?" said Doug, meeting Barbara's gaze with glistening eyes. "I could never forget our baby."

The applause rose as Barbara, Doug and Janee linked arms and headed for the stage, laughing, moving as one, warm and secure in their love—and God's. It was a rare, exquisite moment that Barbara would cherish for the rest of her life.

* * * * *

Dear Reader,

When during my fourth pregnancy I learned my unborn baby had a fatal condition that would claim her life shortly after birth, I wrestled not only with grief but with fear that such a profound loss would sever my close walk with God. Would I be bitter? Would I blame God for letting Misty die? Would I find it hard to trust Him as I had before?

But God was faithful. As a result of that long, hard journey through the shadows—and reality—of death, God gave me a precious intimacy with Him I never could have known outside of grief. The night my daughter died, I felt a tangible awareness of God's presence. It seemed as if Jesus Himself were rocking me to sleep in His arms while His Spirit whispered sweet consolations in my heart. That night I learned a crucial truth that sustains me even today: Better is a time of trial with God's presence than a time of plenty without Him.

As I wrote the story of Barbara and Doug Logan, a couple who after four years are still mourning the death of their five-year-old daughter, I wanted to show how grief can ravage the best of marriages. At a time when couples most need to turn to each other for love and solace, many turn inward and build a wall around their emotions, shutting out the person they need most. Doug turns to his work; Barbara chooses to live in the past. Only through another child—a wide-eyed, curly-haired orphan named Janee—do Doug and Barbara begin to find their way back to each other.

Often, those who grieve shut God out, as well. That is tragic, for He alone is our lifeline when the tides of loss and heartache threaten to drown us. I don't know your losses and heartaches, but I know they are there. You may feel you have no one to turn to, that no one understands. But God does. Jesus loves you with a boundless, immeasurable love, a love that took Him to the cross and delivered Him from the tomb, an unconditional love that accepts you just as you are, this very moment in time. He yearns to gather you into His arms and dry your tears. Please open your heart and let Him love and comfort you.

And remember, I love you, too.

Warmly,

Carole Gift Page

Next month from
Steeple Hill's
Love Inspired®
SECOND TIME AROUND
by
Carol Steward
Dr. Emily Berthoff returned to her hometown to work in a clinic and find the love that had been haunting her for years. Though she had left Kevin MacIntyre to pursue a career in medicine, she knew that something was missing in her life. Would they be able to forgive one another and give their love a second chance?
Don't miss
SECOND TIME AROUND
On sale February 2000
Love Inspired®
LISTA

Starting in February 2000
from Steeple Hill's
Love Inspired®
Discover the lives and loves
of the folks of Fairweather,
Minnesota, in an exciting new
series by three talented authors:
WHAT THE DOCTOR ORDERED
by Cheryl Wolverton
On sale February 2000
TWIN WISHES
by Kathryn Alexander
On sale March 2000
BEN'S BUNDLE OF JOY
by Lenora Worth
On sale April 2000
Love Inspired®
LIFWS